Lynne Markham

Other people and their lives: what shapes them; the influences they are subject to and the effect of these on development and personality, have always held a powerful fascination for me.

Nottingham, the city where I live, is full of interest in this respect: the Huguenot-inspired lace industry; bicycle manufacturing; the tobacco industry – all have played their part in shaping the people and the place, but none more so than Nottinghamshire's coalfield.

Until a few years ago Nottingham was surrounded by mines; you could barely leave the city boundaries without encountering one. Pits and the pit-life were a part of our culture, and there is still a question mark over what will happen now that culture no longer exists.

The Closing March does not pretend to provide the answers, it simply reflects the passing of a way of life, and writing it was for me both a pleasure and a privilege.

Also in the Contents series

Contents

THE CLOSING MARCH

Lynne Markham

mammoth

For Norman

Acknowledgements

I would like to acknowledge the assistance of the Newstead Welfare Band, and of Les and Shirley Ancliff in supplying valuable background information for this book.

First published in Great Britain 1997
by Mammoth
Reissued 2000 by Mammoth
an imprint of Egmont Children's Books Limited,
a division of Egmont Holding Limited
239 Kensington High Street, London W8 6SA

ISBN 0 7497 2876 0

10 9 8 7 6 5 4 3 2 1

A CIP catalogue record for this title
is available from the British Library

Printed and bound in Great Britain
by Cox & Wyman Ltd, Reading, Berkshire

Contents

1 Grandpa

Grandpa ran out of puff on a Sunday. There was a strange sort of noise, like a strangled hen, and then silence.

It was the silence that broke into Mick's train of thought. He held his breath. At the back of his mind he was waiting for B flat to come trumpeting out from Grandpa's room, but instead there was just this eery quiet . . . a dead, empty sort of quiet that muffled the house like a thick white scarf.

'Grandpa?'

Mick's voice came out like the squeak of a mouse. He let his breath out slowly.

'Grandpa?'

Nothing. Nowt. Not even a tiny sound. Not even the sound of his dad snoring in the next room.

Mick felt his toes begin to curl the way they did when he was very frightened. He got out of bed and ran to the door.

'Grandpa!' he yelled.

But there was no reply.

'Grandpa! Grandpa!'

'You can take that look off yer face, young man, I shall say to you what I said to your mam: I'm not dead yet!'

Grandpa was sitting up in bed in his blue-striped pyjamas. There were tufts of grey hair springing out between the buttons on his chest. Grey hair bristled at the base of his neck. In fact, *everything* about Grandpa was bristling. His eyebrows met across his nose. His hair was standing up on end. He looked like a fierce fighting dog Mick had seen once in a picture. His fists were punching into the air. Mick was afraid that he might rear up from his bed at any moment and punch the nearest living thing.

Except that Grandpa could not breathe.

Mick could hear the breath whistling in Grandpa's chest. On his bedside table there was a mask made out of plastic. The mask was attached to a cylinder of oxygen. And next to that was a highly polished soprano cornet.

'And you're not going to stop me from playing her!' Grandpa nodded at the cornet. 'I've been playing her longer than you've been born – and me own pa played her before even that!'

'So maybe you should give it a rest.'

That was Mick's mam speaking, and she always seemed to say the wrong thing. If she had just stayed quiet while Grandpa had his shout, she could have made him do whatever she liked. But she always tried to *manage* him. Grandpa was not the bloke to be managed by her, and even Mick could catch on to that. You had to be one step ahead to get the better of Grandpa, and his mam always seemed to be one step behind.

And now Grandpa was red in the face. His eyes had gone a hard, shiny blue.

'Rest!' he yelled. 'I'll give you rest! I'll march with the lads on closing day and you can damn well make up your minds to that!'

Mick felt himself shrink inside his pyjamas. He could tell that Grandpa was not done yet, but his mam would never see it. She never could spot trouble coming – or not with his grandpa, anyway.

She carried on.

'But you heard yourself what the doctor said. He said you're not to keep on playing that thing.'

'Ho! He did, did he? Well listen here! You can tell your doctor pal what I'm telling you! You don't come up here telling *me* what to do!'

'Pa!'

Mick's mam put a hand across her mouth, as if that might somehow shut Grandpa up. She was staring at him over the hand, and Mick silently willed her to say something back. Grandpa liked you to show a bit of spunk.

But she didn't. Instead, she took her hand very slowly away from her mouth. And then she quietly left the room.

Mick crossed over to the window and drew back the curtains. There was frost on the *inside* of the bedroom window, and the tea towels were frozen to the line. But from every room in the house you

3

could see the pit. The village was dying for want of work, but the pit filled their sights with its great, monstrous bulk.

'I'll clean her for you if you like.'

Mick fingered the cornet on the bedside table. He did not want to play in the band, but he liked the feel of the cold, shiny metal, and the way his face was reflected in it, all long and yellow and ugly.

'Yer not a bad lad, even if you do take after your mam.'

'Shut up, Grandpa, you've said enough. D'you want me to clean her up or not?'

'You've a tongue in your head, our Mick, when you want. Go on then. Take her and give her a rub.'

'And you'll be all right when our Mam comes back up?'

'I'll dazzle her with me wit and charm!'

'You're a bogger, our Grandpa!'

'Language, sonny, language!'

But Grandpa was smiling and wheezing between the smiles. Mick saw him put the mask back on before he closed the bedroom door.

'If you're going outside you're to wrap up warm – and get some sprouts picked on the way back. I want 'em for dinner today though, Mick, so mind you don't go hanging around!'

'You harken to what the Boss says now!' Mr Cotton winked at Mick across the room. 'Do as she says, son, as quick as you can!'

Mick's dad was sprawled at the kitchen table. He was wearing his work overalls although it was Sunday, and there were grease marks along the backs of his hands.

Mick's grandpa did not care for his dad. There was a thing he said when he got really mad: 'You should have took care to marry the gaffer, our Susan, and not set your cap at the oily rag!' But Mick's mam seemed happy enough with his dad, even though he was hardly ever at home. Mr Cotton worked at the local garage, and there always seemed to be a rush-job to do.

Now his mam said, 'You can take this bag with you when you go out – and mind you don't get mud everywhere.'

Mick pulled a face behind her back. His mam always acted sharp like this when she had had a bit of a do with her dad. It was her own funny way of settling back down, and somehow Mick seemed to know that. He knew a lot of things without being told. It was a gift, like being able to draw and paint. Only sometimes it made him uncomfortable. It stopped him from trying to answer her back.

Mick slammed the door and went outside. The allotments were out the back of the house and there was no one around when he first set off. The village was usually quiet now. The only people to stir in the mornings were the young kids on their way to school. Most older folks were laid off work and stayed indoors until later on.

> *'Down in the valley where nobody knows,*
> *Lies Miss Watson without any clothes.'*

Mick sang out loud for company. His breath made a plume of white vapour that floated above his head.

'Down in the valleee where nobody knooows . . .'

It was too cold even to sing. The frost had got into the back of his throat and Mick started to run. He ran down the track as fast as he could with his anorak ballooning out behind. His chest was hurting with the cold, but joy rushed suddenly through his veins like warm, fizzy lemonade, and the day seemed brighter than it had before.

Mick had noticed just lately how his mood kept changing. Ever since Grandpa came to stay he had felt amazingly happy or very sad, without ever knowing the reason why. Now it was enough just to be alive, and he stopped at the end of the track to look round.

The village was where he had spent all of his life and sometimes Mick thought it had changed a lot. At one time the land had been dead flat, but now there were spoil heaps all around that the coal board had moulded into funny round hills. The hills were planted with grass and tiny trees in long, white, opaque plastic tubes. From a distance the tubes looked just like graves – like rows and rows of bone-white tombs.

Mick did not want to think about tombs. In the kitchen at home he had heard his mam talk: 'Pa reckons he's going to march with the band, and what am I going to say to him? You know what he's like when he's set on a thing – he'll never admit he's run out of puff.'

And then Dad's reply: 'Pa does what he wants, love, you know that. If I were you I should just keep quiet and let him sort it out for himself.'

Mick knew what they were talking about. In a few weeks' time the pit in the village was due to close down. And on the last day that it was open for work the brass band would lead the miners out.

Grandpa was a miner and he played in the band, and Grandpa said he was going to march.

Inside his head Mick heard Grandpa's voice: 'I've worked that mine all me flaming life and I'll go out in style with the rest of the lads!'

But Grandpa was iller, and frailer, than he had been before. He would not be fit to march with the band and no one at home dare tell him so. It was a kind of unwritten rule in their house just now that no one must make Grandpa upset.

Mick stayed where he was. He stared at the sky with the thin, black trees in front of it. Grandpa was dying. He knew it, even though it had never been said. It amazed him sometimes that he could be as happy as he was today, when he knew Grandpa would soon be dead.

The sun came out from behind a cloud, and Mick picked some sprouts and turned back home. On the icy ground his feet played a tune, and at the back of his brain he saw Grandpa's cornet, polished and waiting at the side of his bed. Then Grandpa's fierce voice came at him again: 'You're not going to stop me from playing her!'

The cornet meant everything to Grandpa, but it was clear as daylight he could no longer play – and what would happen when he twigged to that? What would happen when he knew for sure that he would not be able to march with the band?

2 The cornet

Blackness and pain. That's how it went. His knees were swelled from being on the ground and sweat made it hard for him to see. He could smell the sweat mixed in with the coal. There was nothing but the jet-black coal and his throat was sour and clogged with it. His head was full of the noise of the trucks rattling along on the lanes behind . . .

'Finish up in five minutes' time!'

Mick sat with his pencil in his hand. He had been making a picture and he could not clear his mind of it. It was as if everything he knew about coal had erupted into life on the page. The shapes fascinated him: the different textures of dark and light. His pencil had moved of its own accord, drawing the blackness inside his head. He was amazed at what he suddenly knew. He wanted to tell somebody about it; for the first time in his life he understood what it had meant to work underground.

'Well done, Mick! That's pretty striking – are you going to show it to your mam?'

'Might do.' Mick shrugged. Miss Watson always spoke as if he somehow needed to be jollied along.

'Or maybe it should go up on the wall?'

Mick covered the paper with his hand. He felt a shrinking embarrassment about his work, as if part of himself was caught on the page for people to stare at, and maybe to laugh at. He did not know why he felt like that – except that what he had drawn was more than a picture; it was his family as far back as it could go. It was a part of his own living past.

Mick put the picture in his bag and quickly drew another. This picture was bland and flat; it showed a miner in an orange hat, and it would blend in with the other work on the wall. He left it on Miss Watson's desk. Mick had the idea that she would like this one; it was simple and clean and easy to look at. Only Mick knew how bad it was. His best work was stored away at home under the spare-room bed, and Mick did not choose to show it around. It would be like giving a part of himself away.

At home time Mick took the long way back. There was a cinder track that wound through the woods and finished up at the end of his road. Officially the track was banned.

'Those woods are dangerous, you don't know who's there.' His mam would be full of the latest news: shallow graves under mounds of leaves, and dead white hands sticking out of the ground.

But Mick needed to be by himself. His brain was jumping and charged with energy. He was seeing things he did not want to see. The pit had got inside Mick's head, without him giving it permission.

He walked on slowly. The woods smelled of toadstools and damp green pine.

Mick had always been afraid of the pit, although he had not told his grandpa that. He was terrified of being shut underground, but with Grandpa so bad he could not tell his mam, and his dad was mostly never there. Mick had to deal with the fear the best way he could.

But the pictures had taken a powerful hold.

And Mick was afraid of the pictures as well as the pit; he had no control over the images that flashed into his mind. A few times before he had been consumed like this: pictures had blazed and flared in his head; he had been gripped by the terror of other creatures, and he had an idea now of what was to come. Last year he had seen the rain-forests go. All summer long his head had been full of smoke and flame and the terrible sound of animals dying.

'That lad of yours has got a skin too few. He's one as takes things much too hard.' A neighbour had said that to his mam when she caught a look at one of his drawings. She reckoned he might have second sight and could talk to the dead if he wanted to. His mam had pooh-poohed that straight away and put it down to the books he read.

But this time Mick put it down to Grandpa. The stories he told were teeming with life. They were full of colour and sound and fury. The stories were nearly as grand as Grandpa himself, and sometimes they made Mick feel very small.

The cinders munched against Mick's boots. It was nearly dark, and the pine trees made an impenetrable pit at either side of the narrow path.

Another thing was weighing on Mick's mind: he was afraid of Grandpa's frailty. As the weeks went by, Mick could see Grandpa's strength slowly oozing away, but nobody ever spoke of it. And, every time he went to visit, it was as if Grandpa's thoughts and dreams and innermost fears were gradually being transferred to Mick.

Mick stopped his walking. The pine woods had come to a sudden end: ahead of him was the village street with yellow lights against the deep blue sky.

Mick felt his insides squeeze together. Outside his house stood the doctor's car.

'Looks like your grandpa's took bad again.' Mr Willis came out from under the lamp and nodded towards the Cottons' door. 'Light's been blazing all day long. Your mam's got a job on her hands, young Mick – you'd best be getting yourself off home.'

'Aye, Mr Willis. Ta, I will.'

But Mick stayed where he was, just staring at the house. Suppose he got home while the doctor was there and found out that his grandpa was dead?

Mick leaned his back against the lamppost and folded his arms across his chest. Usually if he closed his eyes he could shut out the things that bothered him; he could take himself off to a different place he had made inside his head. But since Grandpa took ill he could not do that. If he closed his eyes now, the pictures came . . .

A girder off the jack got him . . .

They had to cut off both his legs . . .

The lamppost struck cold between Mick's shoulders. A mist was curling over the woods. All at once the village looked lost and deserted, full of weird, reproachful ghosts pointing their bony fingers at him.

Mick shivered inside his anorak. He was ashamed of the thing he wanted most: he wanted home to be like it was before Grandpa had come to stay.

When he got home the radio was on, and his mam was in the kitchen. The radio was playing 'Red Roses for a Blue Lady' and his mam was humming along with it. Humming was something his mam always did when things were getting her down; she used the radio like you would use a drug, as a way of shutting out bad things that happened – and today, Mick wished he did not know that.

He put his bag down on the table. 'Hey-up, our Mam! What's going on?'

'Your grandpa's had a bit of a do.'

His mam had to shout above the noise of the music and Mick went to the dresser and switched it off. Upstairs was the rumble-rumble of the doctor's voice and the awful sound of Grandpa's cough.

Mick studied his mam across the kitchen. She had a hand clapped to her face and the other one clutching at her skirt. Her eyes looked very large and dark.

She said to him softly, 'He won't be able to play no more and I'm the one's to tell him that.'

'I expect the doctor's told him already.'

'He won't believe what the doctor says! You know what your

12

grandpa's like by now – he reckons the doctor's a daft young kid –
and he won't believe *me*, you can bet on that!'

Mick wished like mad that his dad was here. It amazed him the
way his dad managed to stay clear of trouble while his mam always
took it face-side up. Mick desperately wanted to help her out, but he
did not rightly know how to begin. He could smell the doctor up the
stairs: that special smell of disinfectant that made his toes curl inside
his shoes.

Mick's fear of doctors had started when he was little and the
doctor had come to watch him walk because of his bandy legs. He
would march into the living-room with his shiny bag and pink, scrubbed
face, and that terrible smell of too-clean hands.

'*Come out, come out, wherever you are!*'

Mick would crouch down low behind a chair, and the doctor would
pretend to search.

'*Ahaa – now – what's this I've found?*'

Mick would be tugged away from his hiding-place. If he closed his
eyes he could still feel the green, woven cottony stuff where his fingers
had clung to the big armchair. He could still smell the dreaded doctor-
smell.

And now one was coming down the stairs!

'Go into the room, our Mick. I'll fetch you when he's gone.'

Mick hid behind the living-room door while the doctor went to talk
to his mam. In his mind the doctor left a ghost behind, with soft white
fingers and a posh brown coat.

'You're stupid,' Mick muttered under his breath. 'You're stupid and you're soft as well.' But talking did not seem to help, and he waited a while in the dark of the hall, and then crept cautiously up the stairs.

The landing light was on and Grandpa's door was standing open.

'You can come on in, young Mick, me lad. Don't stand there dithering like a big, soft girl!'

Mick put his bag down on Grandpa's bed. To his relief Grandpa looked the same as he always did, except that his face was a little bit paler, and his skin looked different in some odd way; it looked thinner, and tighter, as if it was stretched.

'I did something at school for you.'

He took the picture out of his bag and spread it on the bed. From where he stood it looked like a huge, black, gaping hole against the whiteness of the sheets. Grandpa took it up in both his hands.

'By heck, our Mick, you've got me there.'

'We had double art this afternoon, so I did a bloke on the west coalface. He's a stripper, Grandpa, like you told me once. I was drawing it and it all came out! There was the noise, like, and the ache in me back . . . And tomorrow I'm going to do the horse.'

Mick stopped his chatter and looked at Grandpa. The picture was clutched tight in his hands, and Grandpa was staring at it as if he had seen a ghost. The way he looked made Mick think that he had taken himself to another place, and that it was somewhere he did not want to go.

Mick felt stupid for having talked so much; he was one who usually kept things to himself. But this was different. It was as if the past had somehow become massed together to make one hugely powerful, dangerous force. The force was pushing Mick along in a way he could not seem to help. Every nerve-end in his body was charged with the urgent need to draw.

Grandpa sighed very gently, and then put the picture face-up on the bed. For a long moment he did not speak to Mick; he stared out of the window to where the pithead hunched like a vulture against the sky. Then he said quietly, 'I don't know what stuff you're made of, our Mick, but you're a rare one, I can tell you that. This here picture . . . it could be me, years ago, when I were only just a bit of a lad. Just seeing it now . . . it takes me back . . . And tomorrow you're going to do the horse?'

Mick nodded. His skin was hot from what Grandpa said.

'Well, I'll tell you a story about that horse. It happened when I were very young. I were sixteen, give or take a month or so, and a skinny young runty lad for me age. But the ostler – Sam were his name, I think – I'm telling you, Mick, he were a giant of a man!

'And the way things were I'd got this grass. I'd got it from the top of Hobbs field and I was thinking to give the horse a treat. I knew nowt about hosses at that time, and I felt sorry for him living underground, so I fed him the grass – and by gum did he eat! And then next day I go back down for me shift. I'm whistling and acting like I always did – and suddenly I'm lifted up! I'm hooked on the horse's iron collar and me feet's kicking way above the ground!

'What happened was the horse got sick, and grass was what he mainly sicked up. And the ostler, Sam, were roaring away – it were something to see him as mad as that! His face were red and his fists were clenched – I reckon he were as mad as fire! The upshot was he gave me a bucket and I had to clear the whole lot up. I never gave him grass again, and that's the story of the horse, our Mick!'

Mick grinned at Grandpa. The story had made him start to relax.

He said, 'Go on, our Grandpa, you were never sixteen – you don't expect me to believe all that!'

'You watch yer tongue or I'll fetch you a clout!' Grandpa waved his fist across the covers, but he still looked pleased.

'You can keep that picture, if you like, and I'll do you the horse tomorrow.'

'I shall keep it by me bed a while – till your mam comes along to clear it up!'

Mick watched him put the picture on the bedside table. Then he noticed that the cornet was gone. There was a lamp and a glass for Grandpa's teeth, but where the cornet used to stand there was just an empty space.

Mick could not ever remember a time when the cornet was not on the table. Since Grandpa first came to live with them he had kept it firmly within his sights. Mick knew that the cornet was more than just an instrument; it was the thing that told Grandpa who he was.

Grandpa saw the way Mick's eyes were fixed. Very slowly, he said, 'She's in the cupboard where she belongs. I've no blooming use for her any more.'

Mick felt his face begin to bunch together, the way it did when he was going to cry. He stared at the space where the cornet had been.

16

'Maybe you'll get your puff back again. Maybe you'll get it in time for the march.'

'Aye, lad. Maybe you're right about that.'

Neither of them spoke another word. Outside they could hear the doctor's car roaring away from the edge of the kerb. Then the radio was switched back on, and Mrs Cotton began to sing.

Suddenly Mick wanted to get away. He wanted to run and run as far as he could, and maybe never see Bilston again. He went to the door and tugged at the knob.

But Grandpa started to speak again. He said softly, 'The sound of a brass band stays with you, our Mick. You never lose it. I once had a break nearly two years long and there was a hole inside me all that time. It's love, not money, as keeps a brass band going. Maybe you'll have a think on that.'

Mick closed the door and went down the stairs. Then he put his coat on and went outside without even bothering to tell his mam.

3 Paul

At that time of day the street was empty, but there was the smell of dinners cooking: onions and sprouts, and bacon being fried. Mick's stomach grumbled very loudly. He remembered he had not yet had his tea, but he still did not want to go back home.

He crossed the road and went down the alley that led up to the back allotments and the line of houses where his friend, Paul, lived. Paul's house was dark except for a square of light in a thin orange line round the kitchen door.

Mick knocked at the door, and after a minute, Paul came himself.

'You coming on down the line for a bit?'

'If you like. Shan't be a mo.'

Mick stepped in through the kitchen door while Paul went off to fetch his coat.

He looked about him. The kitchen was scruffy and untidy, with stuff just left where it happened to fall. The untidiness did not bother Mick, it made a pleasant change from home: his mam was a stickler for neatness and hygiene, it was something she could not seem to help. But Paul's kitchen was more than just untidy; it was grisly and dripping with blood as well. There was a line strung up across the sink and the line was hung with rabbits. The rabbits were dead and swung by their feet; Mr Reeve would skin them later on.

Mick shivered inside his winter clothes. He tried to avoid the rabbits' eyes. It was January, but it felt like the end of the year: the pit was closing, Grandpa was bad, and the frost outside made your blood run cold.

'Come on, our Mam'll be back in half a tick.'

Paul wore a scarf crossed over his chest and a donkey jacket that belonged to his dad. The jacket nearly reached his knees, the shoulders hung halfway down his arms, and he had the cuffs rolled roughly back.

They set off back down the side of the allotments. Tonight the earth underfoot was crackly with frost, and the stars were out over Hangman's Wood.

'Won't your mam be mad when she finds you gone?' Mick's breath floated about his ears. He felt better than when he first set off.

'Our Mam? Naah! She's her hands full seeing to me dad. He's got himself into one of his moods.'

Everyone knew how bad they were. Sometimes when he was really mad you could hear him roaring streets away.

Mick's mam said, 'That temper goes in the family, his dad were just the same. You want to watch yourself, our Mick, if you keep on taking yourself round there.'

But Mick had never seen Mr Reeve's rage, he had only ever heard it. In his mind he saw an animal, tearing at a cage. The animal was huge and black and hairy and full of a furious, spitting rage. It was a picture that made Mick sorry for Paul; he could not begin to like Mr Reeve. Not even for his best mate's sake.

Mick dug his hands deep into his pockets. From a little way off he heard Paul say, 'She's due down here in two minutes' time.'

They were standing on the railway-line, and there was just the glitter of the stars and the distant glow of the pit. Paul was blowing his nose and coughing a bit; a deep, rattling, chesty cough, that reminded Mick horribly of Grandpa. He was scuffling his feet about in the gravel. There was a lot of litter on the line and Paul was toeing it with the ends of his boots.

Without turning round he said to Mick, 'The quack's been up to your house again.'

'Aye. Me grandpa's bad.'

'It's a wicked business, that it is.' Paul was talking like his dad. 'D'you reckon he'll still get to go with the band?'

Mick shrugged his shoulders and did not reply. He squinted into the middle distance. Some part of him could sense the train before he could properly see it. The way things happened it got into his blood; the blood would thunder and pound in his ears, and then his muscles would start to tense themselves up.

Paul kicked a chip paper out of the way.

'You could learn to play, then you could march yourself.'

Mick did not listen to what Paul said; instead he moved on up the line. He did not want to talk about Grandpa – Grandpa did not belong on the railway-line.

In the distance there was a rumbling noise. Mick strained his ears. There was a yellow pinpoint of light up ahead, and the rumble was getting very loud.

Sometimes Mick nearly wet himself; when the train came near he would clutch his jeans, and that was a thing he did not dare tell Paul. The train reminded him of Mr Reeve: it gave off the same dark, thunderous rage.

'Chicken!' he yelled.

'Chicken yerself!'

The blood was singing in his head and that was the reason why he went. There was always the chance he might freeze to the spot . . . there was always the chance he might not jump.

The afterdraught went up his back.

'By heck, it's made me tabs laugh, that!'

Paul was clinging to the fence. He was laughing like a maniac and wheezing with the laugh. Behind the fence the land ran off to the spoil heaps dotted with plastic tombs. Paul never imagined he might not jump, and somehow Mick seemed to envy him that. Paul never imagined anything much; he saw most things just as a bit of a laugh.

But after the jump there was always the same let-down sort of feeling, like water draining out of a sink. Mick had the notion that he had somehow failed, but he could not fathom the reason why.

'Come on,' he said, 'we'd best get back.'

'But there's another one due in half an hour!'

'You stay if you like, I want me tea.'

'It's no fun doing it on your own!'

They squeezed together under the wire and set off up the frozen track. The air had a strange, metallic tang, as if snow was not very far away. Mick slapped his arms across his chest.

He said to Paul, 'I'll not do it again.'

'What? Go on! You always say that.'

'Only this time I mean it. I'm done wi' the line.'

'Yer yellow, you are! You've a great big streak!'

'Shut up before I clobber you one!'

After that they both stayed quiet. From where he was Mick could hear Paul's breathing. It sounded as if he was going to be sick. Something Paul said was on his mind – that thing about him joining the band.

He said out loud, 'I could play if I wanted.'

They were coming up to the back of Paul's house. It was very quiet and cold and still. They heard a fox scream a long way off.

Paul said, 'You coming in tonight, or what?'

'Naah. Not tonight. There's me tea to have, and one or two things I want to do.'

'Right-oh, then. See you! Ta-ra!'

Mick turned back down the track to his house. There was not another soul about, but he was thinking too hard to be lonely. There was his mam to face when he got back in . . . there was the picture he wanted to draw for Grandpa.

22

**And as well as that there was something else: what if he *did* learn
to play with the band?**

What if he marched instead of Grandpa?

4 Jinty

His snap-tin banged against his hip. This was the part of the day he liked best. Just himself and Jinty on their own. The air was full of Jinty's smell, strong and musty and oddly sweet. 'Come on, lass,' he said under his breath. The back lane was black as your grandfather's hat. He could hear the rumble of Jinty's belly and the distant clonk of the conveyor-belt. If he could stay a ganger he'd fancy that, but he reckoned he'd have to go on the face or risk looking soft in front of his mates. And almost anything was better than that. Even this stupid, crippling fear. He never felt right that far underground. His head was filled with tumbling rocks and his lungs were clogged so he couldn't breathe . . .

'Mick! Mickey! Come on, duck, or you'll be late for school.'

Mick heard his mam down a long, dark tunnel. Part of him was still a mile underground; he was squirming along on his belly. His hands were wrapped round his head; his elbows were skinned and red and sore.

'Mi-ick!'

The picture Mick had drawn was a puzzle to him. It was not what he had meant to draw. There was no horse clomping gently along, no lad leading her down the quiet back lane. It was not the picture he had promised Grandpa.

Mick went to the window and drew back the curtains. It had snowed in the night and the room was flooded with a strange, pale light. The snow had sapped all the colour from the earth, like a sweet that had been sucked too long. Nothing outside looked real any more. Everything was black and white.

Mick held up the picture to the window so that the snow gleamed through.

White on black. Black on white. His stomach twisted into knots. What he had drawn was fear itself; that terrible fear of being underground.

Mick shoved the picture under his pillow and went downstairs to the kitchen. His mam was putting her lipstick on at a little mirror over the sink.

'There's some porridge in the pan, Mick, love.'

Mrs Cotton was wearing her best skirt and blouse. The skirt had a pattern in orange and brown.

'I like your skirt, Mam.'

'Do you, love? Ta. I'll be late tonight, we've got a bigwig coming down, so mind you look after Pa all right.'

Mick stirred at his porridge. He felt a quick, sharp stab of disappointment. He wanted to talk to his mam about Grandpa – about what he was like when he was young.

Because suddenly there were two Grandpas: the stroppy one upstairs in bed, and the one he had drawn, who was more like Mick – this other Grandpa who was afraid of the dark.

Mick said, 'Grandpa shouldn't talk to you like he does.'

'Eh? What's brought this on then, our Mick? You know your grandpa's always been the same.'

'He hasn't! Not always! He were not like that when he were a lad!' Mick stopped abruptly and bit his lip.

But now Mick had got his mam's attention. She stayed where she was with her hand in the air, and looked at him through the mirror.

'What's the matter with you, Mick? Have you got a pain somewhere? Have you got another one of your heads?'

Mick could not tell his mam the truth. He threw down his spoon and yelled over the table, 'Why do you think I've got a pain when all I want is to talk to you?'

Mrs Cotton put the lipstick away. She did it very slowly and thoughtfully. Then she came to the table and looked down at Mick.

She said, 'You mustn't fret about me and your grandpa. He doesn't mean the half of what he says. It's just that . . . I disappointed him. He always thought he should have fathered lads because that's the way it used to be – lads gave you clout, they carried on the family name. In them days folks didn't want just girls.'

'Yeah, well . . . I'll pop up and see him before I go.'

'I shouldn't, my duck, if I were you. He's having a sleep – and any road up, it's time that you were off to school. Don't forget to take your snap-box with you – your wellies are behind the kitchen door.'

Mick pulled on his boots and went outside. The white snow made everything look fresh and soft and very clean, so that even the pit-head looked like art.

He walked very fast with his hands in his pockets. The snow made him think of being abroad, like those pictures he had seen in magazines. It made him think how small Bilston was, and that one day he might leave it for good.

But first he had to get through school.

And at school the pit was everywhere. They were doing a project on the history of mines in the form of a mural to go up in the hall. On the day the mine was closed for good, the school would be open to the public to go and look at their work. Mr Riley announced the project that morning in one of his regular talks to the school. Mr Riley was short and tubby and red in the face. Rumour had it he wore special shoes. He had a purple nose and not much hair – but somehow you listened to Mr Riley.

The project was for all the school: '. . . I want you to show the world,' he said, 'that we're not just fodder for shovelling coal. I want you to show that we're people as well, with talent and ideas to give to the world . . .'

Mr Riley thought the TV men would come and put them on the *Nine O'clock News.* He thought the school would be famous then. There would be photographs taken, and the Lord Mayor would arrive.

The day would be like a festival; full of excitement and celebration. Everyone had their own ideas about what they wanted from the mine.

Only Mick was not easy in his mind. There was a question he wanted to ask Mr Riley, but he could not rightly think of the words.

Mick sat where he was with his chin in his hands. Outside the sun was melting the snow; but inside the hall there was something wrong. Mick was angry with Mr Riley.

Grandpa was seen as factory fodder. Fodder was something you gave to cows!

And now Grandpa's cornet was put away, shrouded in linen as if it was dead.

Mick thought it was as if Grandpa had put *himself* away in a cupboard. Grandpa was not the man Mick had thought he was; he was smaller, and at the same time, larger, somehow. Everything was changing much too fast; Grandpa, the village, the way his own thoughts ran. What if he, Mick, could not catch up? What if the world went careering past, and Mick was the one who got left behind?

Later that day Mick drew a horse.

The horse was a faded brown against the black of the dark back lanes. And beside the horse there was a boy. The boy was very tall and thin; his face was just a speck of white. Mick remembered what his grandpa said: he said he had been tall when he was a lad. Tall and thin like a stout ash pole – and that was before he got miner's squat.

Mick studied the drawing. He thought it was both soft and hard. The boy looked a little bit like himself, as if he was reflected back in it.

He put the picture in his bag and went home by the fastest route. When he got in, the house was quiet. Snow was gleaming through the living-room windows, and Mick took the picture out again and propped it against the mantelpiece.

The horse and the boy looked startlingly alive. In his mind he could hear them shuffling along; the grunting breath and the swish of a tail. He could smell the leather on the cracked black harness, and the rich, ripe stench of horse manure.

Another picture came into his mind: over the top of the horse and the boy, there was a woman standing by the pit's main gate. Mick could not properly see her face, but he had the impression of enormous strain, and a shocking, gut-wrenching sense of fear. Her body was leaning towards the pit, and the pit was flooded with bright white light.

Mick covered his eyes. He did not want the pictures to come, but he did not know how to stop them.

He went upstairs to his grandpa's room with the picture of the horse and the boy in his hand. When he knocked on the door there was dead silence.

He knocked again. More silence.

He stuck his head round the bedroom door.

'Look, Grandpa! Look what I've done!'

Grandpa was just a thin white lump with a tuft of hair on the pillow. The sheet was not moving up and down. Mick could not see any signs of life.

His heart gave a single, deafening thump.

The top of his head began to tingle, and when he tried to move

29

he found that he couldn't. Mick was on his own with Grandpa. There was no one to help him; his dad would be at the garage until late; his mam was not due back at home for at least another half-hour.

Mick stared at the shapeless lump on the bed. It did not look human any more.

Mick leaned forwards slightly. He discovered that he could not properly breathe, and a big, hard lump was in his chest. Very slowly he let out his breath, and at the same time, a thin white plume of smoke spiralled upwards from the bed.

'Grandpa!'

Grandpa's face came out from under the sheet. His mouth was puckered into a tight black darn with spidery stitches at either side. The skin on his face was deep brick-red from the effort of trying to hold his breath.

'Grandpa!' Mick shouted. 'You've been smoking again! After what you promised – I thought you was dead! I can smell them flaming fags from here! Honest, Grandpa, I could murder you! Give it to me – come on, hand it over – you know what Mam has to say about that . . . And she only gets what she says from the quack.'

Fear made Mick's voice louder and harsher than it usually was, and now Grandpa's eyes were starting to water. He opened his mouth and a thick cloud of smoke floated out across the bed. When the smoke was gone he started to cough.

Mick said more quietly, 'I'll not be sorry for you having that cough! You know fine what the doctor said!'

And Grandpa moved his hand out from under the sheet. There

was a cigarette cupped in the palm of it. Very deliberately he put the cigarette in the kidney-shaped bowl at the side of his bed. Then he said softly, 'Don't go on at me like that, young man. It ain't right for me, and it ain't right for you – and any road up, whatever I do you know it's no use – you know I'm done for, like it or not. You know I'm killed already.'

Mick could not keep his anger up. It was not up to him to decide what was right, or to give Grandpa lip the way he had.

He sat down on the edge of the bed and handed his picture over to Grandpa.

'Look at this – something I did at school today. Maybe it'll make you feel better.'

'You can draw a lot better than you can sing – I heard you cater-wauling the other night!'

'I know that right enough, our Pa . . . now tell me what you think of it.'

Grandpa put his spectacles on his nose and studied the picture carefully. Then he held it up to the lamp, so that the light shone through.

He said to Mick, 'I think it's grand, lad, that I do. I can very nearly smell that 'orse. Jinty her name was. She was right as ninepence, and frisky as owt, but she were a bit of a beggar for stealing your snap. She could lift the lid of yer snap-tin fast, and you'd never know the difference – not until you came to eat it, like . . . And as well as that she could count an'all. She'd only pull three wagons at a go. The way things were she'd listen for clunks and she'd not move an inch if she counted four.'

'What happened to her in the end?'

'I don't know as I can answer that. I weren't a ganger for very long. I were shifted to the dogging-on. But I missed that 'orse – I cried for her, Mick, I'll tell you that. She were a friend to me when I needed one. There was just the two of us down there in the dark. She were another living thing, d'you see?'

Mick did see. And for the first time in his life he saw himself clearly in Grandpa. Up until then Mick had been very careful that Grandpa should not find him out. Grandpa was always so big and strong; there was no doubt that Grandpa was one of the lads. But Mick was an artist and a dreamer. He suspected he might be a bit of a wimp, and that Grandpa might despise him for that.

He said now, 'What'd you have done if it weren't for the pit?'

And the question made Grandpa go very quiet. His face had a strange, folded-in sort of look, as if his thoughts went very deep. Then all at once he gave a sigh.

He said, 'I had a fancy to go and work on the land. You see, Bilston were very much smaller then. It had more of a feel of the countryside. And there was a keeper as worked for Bilston House. He'd say, "I shall want you, Brown, on Saturday morning." We used to go beating for the shoot – me and Billy Drayton – ten bob and your dinner was what you got. There'd be a pie the size of I don't know what wi' ten rabbits standing up in it. I got to thinking that keeper might take me on – he were a grand chap for all the airs he'd got – but nothing ever came of it.'

And so Grandpa had gone down the pit instead.

Mick looked out of the window. The pit was a huge, black, bottomless hole that swallowed the local villagers up. It was the best and the worst of all he knew. All that they had came out of the ground: jobs for the boys when they left school; work for the girls up at Coal House.

And now the pit was closing down.

Mick could not even begin to feel sorry. He might have been processed into the pit and that would have been the way his life went. Now, a whole new world would open up. Now, he could be whatever he liked.

He said to Grandpa, 'Can I have a blow on your cornet?'

'Not just now, lad. I've put her away.'

Mick suddenly felt very shy. He wanted to ask Grandpa about the march – but what if he did and he got upset? Mick felt closer to Grandpa than ever before, but he could not be sure how he might react.

In the end it all came out in a rush. He said, 'Why don't you let me go and play for you? I could learn the cornet quick as owt, and then I could go and march with the band.'

Grandpa did not make a reply straight away. Instead, he snatched the mask off his bedside table and breathed in very deeply. And all the time he was breathing he was looking close at Mick. When he had got his breath back again, he said, 'Play the cornet? You? Get on with you, lad! You know right well you're tone bloomin' deaf!'

'And that's all you know! It's only me voice! You're just saying that because you know I can't sing!'

'And there's more to playing than just blowing a bit! Come over here lad, where I can see.'

Mick moved up closer to where Grandpa was. He was stung by what he had said ... Of course he could play the stupid cornet! Practically everyone he knew could do that!

Grandpa said, 'I know what you're thinking, but it's not like that. It takes time to get inside an instrument – and it takes even longer to get into a band. Listen to me, Mick. There's lads been waiting years for a chance to have a go with the band – and they're the pick of the kids around. I wouldn't want you to go letting me down.'

Mick felt his face go a steamy red. He knew the way Grandpa's thoughts were turning, and the old confusion came flooding back. Somehow being Mick was not good enough. Mick was not like the other lads – and neither was he enough like Grandpa.

'I don't want to go upsetting you, son.' Grandpa touched Mick's arm. His fingers felt very soft and smooth, like a young girl's skin, or a very old man's. But Grandpa was only sixty-five. It was being laid off from work as long as he had that made his skin go smooth like that.

Now Mick said, 'I *could* play, Grandpa, if I got the chance – or nobody from our house will go with the band.'

Grandpa moved his head against the pillow and stared out of the window. It looked as if he was thinking very long and hard, and that the thinking did not come easy. Then he said to Mick, 'I shall have a word with Charlie Binns. He's by way of being a mate of mine. I'm not promising owt will come of it – but if he takes you on, you'll have to work. You'll not go letting the Brown side down.'

Mick grinned at Grandpa. 'I'll blow till me eyes fall out of me head! Now, where do you want me to put the horse?'

'Put it on the wall at the end of the bed. I want to be able to see it.'

Mick Blu-tacked the picture on to the wall – his mam would go mad if he left any marks. Next to the horse was the man on the coal-face. Mick liked the way they were side by side. Grandpa's life was turning into a story, and it was a better story – happier and sadder and richer somehow, than Mick had ever thought.

5 The audition

No one told him it would be like this. They hadn't warned him about the cold. It was that cold it took your breath away and his gloves were stuck to his hands with ice. And all the time the trucks kept coming. He was coupling trucks together all day. It was what the lads called dogging-on. But he missed the horse and the lonely quiet; he kept on wondering how she was doing. And then the wind blew down his back and he nearly let the trucks run past. His hands were too cold to find the wedge; he couldn't stop them running off.

It was worse than he ever thought it would be. The freezing cold, the wind and the wet. And tomorrow he'd have to do it again . . . And the day after that . . . And the day after that . . .

Mick woke up shivering with the cold. Even his hands were freezing cold and his face was covered with stone-cold sweat.

Only the butterflies seemed to give out warmth. Mick looked at the butterflies on his bedroom ceiling. Ten of them with outstretched wings fluttering across the hint of peach. The one he liked best was a Peruvian Marcellus with long floating wings in red and purple. He had painted it on a jungle leaf with spiky edges and make-believe flowers of magenta and mauve. If he narrowed his eyes in a certain way the butterflies and the leaf and the giant pink flowers seemed to move across the ceiling as if they were moving through the jungle.

'A right little Michelangelo,' his mam had said. 'Just mind that paint on your nice bedspread.'

But she had stared at the ceiling for a very long time.

Now the butterflies seemed to draw Mick in. He was in the depths of the jungle, floating in the rich, dark green.

Except today was the day he would see Charlie Binns. Mick had met Charlie Binns a few times before when he came to the house to see Grandpa. That was when Grandpa could still get about, before his breathing got so bad. His mates would come round to cheer him up and it would be party time in Grandpa's room. Mick would lie in bed and listen to the noise. It amazed him that Charlie Binns could sing. He had a husky, smoked-kipper sort of voice. He had a belly that wobbled when he laughed, and Mick's mam did not like him much, but Mick did not know the reason why.

Whenever Charlie's name cropped up her face would get That Look again. It was a tight-lipped, I-won't-say-anything-rude sort of look, that was worse than if she had spoken out loud.

And tonight Charlie was coming here!

Mick's hands went clammy; he would have to try and please Charlie Binns at the same time as trying to please his mam.

And that night his mam stayed at the kitchen table, knitting a jumper in thick red wool. The jumper had a pattern like rows and rows of tiny teeth, and occasionally she would stop to count her stitches and point at the pattern with a long, shiny pin.

But she never mentioned Charlie Binns.

It was as if Mick had somehow made him up and he did not exist except inside his head. He wanted to draw Charlie with his black-treacle eyes and the belly he got from drinking beer. He wanted to prove to himself that Charlie was real. But instead he was drawing a bunch of flowers, and the flowers were a way of trying to please his mam.

When she saw the pictures on Grandpa's wall Mam had looked away very quickly. She said, 'Can't you draw something a bit more lively, love? It gives me the creeps to look at them.'

Mick was hurt by what she said. He wanted her to see the amazing story that was slowly and carefully taking shape. If she looked at the pictures properly, she might understand how special it was. But, 'Draw me a bunch of roses,' Mam said. 'Draw me something I can nearly smell.'

The flowers Mick drew were odd, twisted shapes, nothing at all like roses. They had long, thin petals that were covered with spots and stamens that looked like bloody red fangs.

Mick was scowling at the picture and wishing he could talk to his

38

mam. He was afraid that he was moving away from her; that by joining the band he would be taking sides and lining up alongside Grandpa.

But Mick kept quiet. He stayed where he was with the horrible flowers, and at eight o'clock there was a knock at the door. It was a loud and very firm rat-a-tat-tat.

Mick waited for his mam to answer the knock, and she must have heard it right enough, but she did not bother to look up from her knitting.

The second knock was louder than the first: *Rat-a-tat! Rat-a-tat! Rat-a-tat-tat!*

Mick broke the tip off his pencil. He glanced at his mam. What would she do if he mentioned Charlie? What would *he* do if she never got up to answer the door?

Outside in the porch there was a scuffling noise, like boots being cleaned and scraped on the mat. A second later the letterbox rattled.

'Come on, missus!' Mick heard Charlie shout. 'It's cold as blooming Christmas out here! Open the door if you're going to!'

Mick glanced towards his mam again, then he said very softly, 'What's to do, our Mam? Am I to go and let them in?'

And his mam laid her knitting down on her knee. Her hands were smoothing it over and over. Mick was afraid she would not answer his question, but just carry on stroking the jumper as if it was a cat.

He waited, and his mam said suddenly, 'Answer the door if you must, our Mick, but make sure you take them straight upstairs.'

Charlie Binns was waiting with two of his mates and a plastic bag with bottles of beer. When Mick opened the door they surged inside.

'Now then, Mick, so how's yer mam?'

'Hey-up, Mrs Cotton, we've come for yer dad!'

'Are you going to fetch us some glasses then, Mick?'

They swept Mick up in front of them.

'Watch out, young Charlie, drunk again!' A mate cuffed Charlie round the ear. He grinned.

'It's the sight of you makes me fall about!'

The men made Mick think of big, clumsy dogs with enormous feet and wagging tails. Mick's mam and the funny mood she was in seemed to fade away when the men came in.

Grandpa was sitting up in bed. He was properly dressed, his hair was brushed, and his pyjamas were clean and pressed and spruce. The excitement had brought a flush to his face and he looked better than Mick could remember him looking since the day he first came to live with them.

Charlie was shouting out to Grandpa, 'How-do then, Gil? I thought you was ill! Cop a look at this, lads – have you ever seen him look so well?'

'It's knocked me duck off, seeing you!'

'Is them pyjamas you might be wearing? Or are they by way of being a frock? By gum, Gil Brown, you're spruce as a gell!'

Mick stayed where he was and listened to the chaff. There was something about the men that made you want to be with them. At school Mick did not have many friends. But tonight with Grandpa and his mates acting up, he had a queer sense of things being pushed out of shape. He kept looking at the men with their pit-pale faces and rings of black inside their nails. He had thought he did not want to be like them, but now, all at once, he was not so sure.

They got to talking about the mine, and what they would do when it closed for good.

'I'm too old to train for owt much else.'

'Me missus'll have to bring the brass in.'

'I hear they want blokes up Cardale Pit.'

'Aye – and you'd be out on your ear in a month or two!'

There was a sudden silence in the room. Nobody said what they wanted to say: that most of the men would never find work; that their wives would have to find work in the town; that you could not shop in the village now, because the corner shops had all closed down.

Charlie and his mates stared into their beer. For a long moment nobody spoke.

Then at last Grandpa gave a rasping cough.

He said, 'Our Mick's one as can draw a bit. Take a look at them pictures on the wall, and see if they don't take you back.'

Mick buried his face in his glass of beer. The beer was thick brown bottled stuff with a creamy head on top of it. His mam would kill him if she knew what was what, and Mick had the idea the beer was taking effect. The pictures on the wall looked blurred round the edges, and he was hearing the talk from a long way off.

'By gum, Mick, where d'you get it from?'

'That's you, Gil, there! It's plain as plain!'

'How does he know what it were like?'

'Will he do one for me to put on the wall?'

Mick's head was spinning round and round, and then: 'Hey-up lads, watch it, he's going to be sick!'

The floor came up in a fuzzy wave. Mick could see the wool of the bedroom carpet in a strange, close-up, whiskery weave. The wool was covered in thick grey ash, dotted about with splashes of beer. The last thing Mick could remember thinking was, our Mam'll go barmy when she comes up to clean!

Mick's mam said, 'Men – you're all the same!'

His dad said, 'Leave the lad alone.'

Mick was in bed and his mam was wiping his face with a cloth. She was none too careful as to how she did it and the icy water got into his eyes.

'Ow! Stop that, will you? I'm OK now!'

'Don't go giving me your lip – the state you were in when I found you last night!'

'Lads'll be lads, Susan. You know that.'

Mick's dad was proud of him for being so sick. Ever since breakfast he had been hanging around, trying to save Mick from his mam. But Mick's mam was angry out of all proportion to what had gone on.

And now Mick pushed her roughly away. He shouted at her, 'Leave me, will you? I'm not a kid – and I'm telling you I'm OK now!' He was anxious to go and see Grandpa again, to find out if he could play with the band. Last night was just a blur to Mick.

It might have been the beer again, but before he woke up Mick had had a dream. He dreamed of a woman by the main gate, and she stared out of the dream straight into his eyes. Mick could not begin to think who she was, and yet she was vaguely familiar. There was something about the shape of her face that made him think he had seen her before. He might make a drawing later on, and see if Grandpa could give her a name.

Grandpa's room still smelled of beer, but it was mixed in with the smell of disinfectant, and the sweet, powdery smell of carpet shampoo. The room was neat and tidy again, but it had an angry, implacable look, as if Mam's mood had rubbed off on it. Even Grandpa looked subdued. His face was pale and tinged with grey and he was lying very straight in bed.

'Grandpa! Did you ask Charlie Binns last night about me going to play with the band?'

'You don't muck about when you want sommat!'

'Aye, I know that, Grandpa. It's something as I learned from you.'

'Cheeky bogger! I *did* have a word with Charlie Binns, and you're to go down Welfare Hall tonight. He's only going to give you a test, so mind you don't get your hopes too high.'

'Ta, Grandpa. I'll do me best.'

'I expect you will, so I'll say no more.'

Grandpa sighed as if it hurt him to sigh, and after that they both stayed quiet. Mick was too groggy to go to school and his mam had written him a note. Her pen had made angry marks on the page, and she had written what she called a Little White Lie.

Mick sat on a chair at the side of Grandpa's bed with his elbows resting loose on his knees. Ever since he had first got up he had been feeling vaguely unhappy. It was not just the drink that had got to him, or even the way his mam had behaved. There was something teasing at the back of his mind; something he could not quite recall. He had the idea Mr Riley was there, and that it was something important to do with cows . . .

Mick was so sunk into his own dark thoughts he hardly heard what Grandpa said next. He was talking very soft and low, as if he had forgotten Mick was there.

Grandpa said, 'It's times like this when I miss Doris most. She was a good lass, Doris – one of the best.'

Grandpa's wife had died when she was very young and Mick was still a baby. Grandpa did not speak of her all that much – Mick's mam said the loss had cut him up – but now that he had started to speak again, it was as if he could not bear to stop.

Grandpa carried on: 'I met her when we were both sixteen. I used to go courting wi' the other lads. Sunday night we'd go after chapel – we each had a stile or a fence or a post – and that's where we'd do our courting. I were a skinny, ugly chap, but Doris – she were well set up! She caught the eye of all the lads and I were flattered to death when she landed on me. Only I weren't in a hurry for us to get married. I still had this thought of going on the land. My head was full of what I might do . . . I couldn't seem to settle for going down mine.

'But Doris – she got tired of waiting! Her pals were all getting married off. So she says to me, "I'll be over tonight, and we'll go to see the parson." The upshot was we were married in June – and that parson hadn't a hair on his head! He were a great big fellow in spite of that – but imagine – without a single hair!'

At seven o'clock Mick left the house without telling his mam what he was going to do. His mam had come home from work quite late and her face had looked very puffy and pale. She was too tired even to be mad at him.

And tonight the village was as quiet as the grave. The mist swirled about Mick in a thick, white cloud. There was no one about for company.

Bilston was a shadow town. The stars were hidden behind the cloud, and the only noise was a distant train rumbling down the Robin Hood line. Then the Welfare Hall loomed out of the mist. Its windows were orange squares of light that turned the mist into mustard soup. Hangman's Wood leaned over the village, a darker shape behind the fog.

Mick stood in the shadow at the side of the door. Now that he was here he was feeling afraid. The idea that he could play with the band seemed foolish and stupid beyond belief. He remembered Grandpa's words to him: *I'll not have you go letting me down.* And some of what Grandpa said was true: Mick had no talent for music, music came third after nature and art. The patterns it made appealed to him, but it was not the same as drawing things; Mick felt happier and more in charge when he had a pencil in his hand.

The band was bigger than Mick remembered; he could see it through the window. There was Charlie Binns in a circle of men. From where he was standing Mick could hear the band and the noise of

Charlie shouting. Then the tuba played a long, low note, and that was a bleak and lonely sound.

The door swung open suddenly; there was a waft of beer and cigarettes.

'Hello, young Mick! What you doing here?'

'I've come to try out for the band.'

'You'd best hop inside then, out the cold.'

Mick stepped inside the corridor. The walls were painted a pale pea-green; there were adverts up for Mansfield Bitter, and a list of fixtures for the local darts team. Inside the hall there was a bar that ran the length of one of the walls; the bar was covered with a metal grille, and at the end of the hall there was a stage. The band was sitting in front of the stage and Charlie was doing the talking: 'Are you holding back deliberately, George? Can you take it again from number three?

'Don't give me that, John, hold it longer – no, youth, not like a flaming cow – this isn't a funeral you're playing for . . .'

Mick stayed where he was and looked at Charlie. Charlie looked taller, and older, and not so fat. Even his voice had changed and grown deeper; he talked like you do when you know you're in charge and none of the others will answer back. Watching Charlie, Mick knew for sure that music was something you did for love – Grandpa had spoken the simple truth, and Mick had not understood it right.

One of the band had spotted Mick, and was digging his neighbour in his side. They grinned and waved, and Mick waved back, then Charlie Binns turned round.

'I'll be with you, Mick, in half a tick. I just want to get this new bit straight.'

The band was finished in a couple of minutes. Chairs were being scraped on the wooden floor and there was the buzz of people talking. One or two blokes called out to Mick, 'How's your grandpa doing then, young Mick? Is he managing to get around?'

Charlie was shouting at the men, 'Ten minutes and we start again.'. Then he came up to Mick and pinched his chin. 'Don't look so scared. I won't bite yet – not till you make me really mad!'

Mick's heart sank down into his shoes. He gazed at the pattern on Charlie's jumper, like a row of rabbits hand in hand. Now that he and Charlie were on their own, he could not think of a thing to say. He cleared his throat.

'Mr Binns,' he said, from a long way off, 'I reckon I've been and made a mistake – I reckon I'll not try to play with the band. And our Mam'll be wondering where I am, so I'll be getting off home now, if you don't mind.'

The way Mick's voice slipped out of his mouth was as if it had got a life of its own. He was glad now that he had not told his mam where he was – it would be bad enough having to explain things to Grandpa, without having to talk it out with her.

But Charlie Binns took hold of his arm. 'Got the collywobbles, son? Come in here where we can have some quiet.'

They moved out of the hall and into a room furnished with big, sagging, scruffy armchairs, and a fruit-machine that was all lit up.

There was a telly under the biggest window, and a tall, blue cupboard against the wall.

Charlie unlocked the cupboard and took out a cornet. It was not as shiny as Grandpa's cornet, but it had the colour of wedding-ring gold.

Charlie balanced the cornet in his hands. He stroked it gently for a second or two, and then carefully handed it over to Mick. 'Here you are then, lad,' he said. 'Moment of truth! Let's see if you can give us a blow!'

Mick's fears came back like a flock of crows. Supposing he could not make a noise? Charlie would think he was a big, soft girl – though come to think of it, there were girls in the band!

He took the cornet and sucked in his breath. And then he blew it out as hard as he could. He blew and blew until his face went red, but he did not manage to make a sound!

The room went very quiet after that. Mick could hear his own breath inside his chest. He could not believe what had happened to him – after all the chat he had given to Grandpa, *he* was the one without any puff! He gazed at the grain of the wooden floor, but what he saw was the march going by. There was the noise and the smell of the local crowd, cameras flashing on and off and the glint of the sun on the big trombone.

All that would happen without him now – and Charlie Binns was laughing!

His belly was rippling with the laugh, and his eyes had vanished into two deep folds. When he had finished the laugh he wiped his eyes and took the cornet from Mick's cold hand. He blew into it once, one clear, loud note. Then he handed the cornet back to Mick.

'There now,' he said. 'We'll start again. It's not just puff you want wi' that. It's all to do with the lips and tongue. I want you to buzz against the mouthpiece and make your lips shake like they do when you cry. Or think you've a tea leaf stuck on your tongue and you're doing your damnedest to spit it out!'

Mick tried again, and a sound came out like a very loud snore.

'You're nearly there, youth! Try again – and remember to use them lips of yours.'

Mick was Charlie's best mate's grandson – and maybe that's why he was being so kind. Mick glanced at Charlie from the side of his face and then looked away again at once.

He said, 'It's no use, Mr Binns! I'd best give up.'

And Charlie's face went a bright, steaming red.

'Give up?' he yelled. 'You what? Did I hear wrong? Or do me ears want washing out? I thought – correct me if you like! – that you was grandson to Gilbert Brown.'

Mick took out a handkerchief and blew his nose.

Then Charlie smacked his hands together. 'That's the noise I want to hear! Now blow us a blinder like you blew your nose!'

Suddenly Mick forgot to be shy. He grinned at Charlie. 'Right then,' he said. 'Get your ears pinned back! I'm going to blow her properly now.'

The mouthpiece was shiny and wet with spit. Mick wiped it carefully on his sleeve. The cornet had a cold, pale-yellow taste that made Mick think of slippery fish. He took his time adjusting it. The brass was rattling against his teeth, and then he took another deep breath. The note that came out was loud and clear and in perfect tune, like the sound of a seagull crying.

Charlie slapped him hard across the back. 'Well done, lad! That's the stuff I want to hear! Now see if you can do it again.'

Mick blew a note the same as the last.

'Good lad! That's *your* note, that is. Whenever you hear that noise coming out you'll know right enough as you're playing B flat.'

Charlie took the cornet away from him and put it in a cloth. He wrapped it slowly and carefully, and then he handed it back to Mick.

'Here you are then, Mick. This is yours now, lad, for as long as you want to keep it. You have to look after it properly, mind, and make sure you keep it squeaky clean. And another thing while you're here, young man! I shall see you at our house tomorrow at six.'

'You're going to teach me how to play?'

Charlie winked at him, and tapped his nose. 'Aye – and don't go looking at me like that. There's weeks of hard work for you, me lad. And there'll be times when you wish you'd never been born!'

Mick tucked the cornet under his arm. He walked outside with his hands in his pockets and the cornet pressed close against his ribs. There was an idea that things were coming together in a way that was slow and natural.

Grandpa and the band and Charlie Binns. They were like a pattern in his head. He was finding a way to make sense of things: the day that the pit closed down for good he would march with the miners instead of Grandpa. He would work as hard as Charlie said – and he would not be letting the Brown side down!

6 Lesson one

It was kept so cold to keep the gas away, and that was something he understood – but as well as the gas there were the men to keep cool. A bloke sweat cobs way out at the face, crouched in the dark with a few of his mates. It was twenty degrees colder inside the pit, but the men on the face got lathered with sweat; only the doggers got the full blast of cold, and sometimes he was the only one.

He never thought he would be so lonely. It wasn't the same as being with the horse. This was a different kind of lonely, where you couldn't imagine yourself anywhere else . . . because your hands and your feet and your brain went numb and it took all your strength to keep dogging on . . .

Mick's picture was just a dead black square with a white line running through the middle. The way his pencil had moved over the page had taken him by surprise. He had meant to draw something to go up in the hall; something clean and simple you could recognise. But instead he had come out with a big black square: a dense and ugly life-sapping hole. He had the sense of the walls closing in, and the ceiling coming further down.

Mick crouched over his picture. He was starting to feel a bit sick inside and his hands were freezing cold. He was sitting in the warm at Bilston School, but his brain was trapped in the cold and the dark. There was a yearning for the scut of a rabbit's tail, and the rich brown earth instead of coal.

'What's the matter with you, Mick? Are you feeling poorly?'

'No, sir, thanks, sir. I'm all right now.'

'Well, let's see what you've been up to, then.'

The room came sharply back into focus. Mick did not want anyone else to see what he had drawn. But Mr Brierly was in charge of the mural that was gradually going up round the hall.

The mural irritated Mick. It showed the miners from the beginning, right up until the present day. There were mosaic people with picks in their hands and mucky coal-black faces. There was even some winding gear in papier-mâché that moved round and round when it caught the breeze. Every child in the school had made something and the mural would stay there for months to come. Mr Riley was pleased with the way it was shaping; he kept popping out into the hall to look, and then rubbing his little pink hands together and telling them all to keep it up.

Only to Mick did it look unreal. The figures stuck up on the wall with glue were nothing like the ones inside his head. They only showed you what people *did*, they did not show you what they were.

To see what people were really like you would have to look at the pictures on Grandpa's wall. Mick was not conceited about what he had done, he just *knew* that somehow he had got it right. Grandpa had Mick's pictures arranged in a line, so he could see them properly when he lay in bed. He kept saying to Mick it was like seeing the past come back to life in front of your eyes.

'They say it's what happens when you croak!'

'Get off, our Grandpa, you're not going to die!'

'We've all got to go, son, sooner or later. It's one of them pesky laws of nature . . . and these here pictures, they bring things back. It's like being meself again when I was young, only knowing all the things I think I know now. It's a right strange sort of feeling. I can't say it to you properly; it's like being happy and full of yourself, and at the same time being sad.'

Mick was remembering what Grandpa said while Mr Brierly waited.

Very slowly he moved away from his picture. It emerged from under his arm like a hole opening up, and Mr Brierly stared at it.

It was a long, silent stare, like you get before an explosion. Mr Brierly was a man who often exploded if someone got across him. His body would seem to puff itself up like a cobra waiting to strike. There would be a moment of hush, and then he would yell, 'Stop what you're doing, you malfunctioning clod! Then come over here and get a thick ear!'

The way Mr Brierly yelled you would expect the kids to be scared of him, but it did not quite work out like that. Mr Brierly was like a volcano exploding *Bang*! *Bang*! *Bang*! and then it was over and done with for good. Mr Brierly got mad and yelled at you, but he never really made you feel small.

Mick waited for the explosion. But instead Mr Brierly puffed out his breath. It made a long, slow, whistling noise. Then he put a hand on Mick's shoulder. He said, 'I want you to tell me all about this. Come over here where we can have some quiet.'

He went over to a space behind his desk and Mick trailed after. Mr Brierly spread the picture out in front of him. He treated it very carefully, as if it was a precious work of art, and then he cocked an eyebrow up at Mick.

'You can draw, Mick Cotton,' he said, 'and I don't mean you can knock up a line or two – any daft clod in school can do that. I mean you've got talent, son, real talent, and I'm not sure I can follow you down that road. Me, I'm just a teacher, I can't make anything special myself. But you . . . what have we got in front of us, lad? Tell me, will you? I want to know.'

Mick would have preferred Mr Brierly to be angry. But instead he sounded awe-stricken, as if he somehow had to be careful of Mick! Being flattered and embarrassed was new to Mick; he did not know what to do with it.

'Mr Riley said the old blokes were fodder! Fodder's sommat you give to cows! But this here's what it were really like, stuck for miles under the chuffing ground!'

Mr Brierly folded his arms across his chest and waited a while for Mick to calm down. Then he gave another of his deep, whistling sighs. He said, 'I can understand what you're saying to me, Mick. My old man was a miner too. I'm the one as got away, and maybe I didn't get far enough! But listen to me a minute, young man – I reckon you've got Mr Riley wrong. He wasn't saying as miners were fodder, he was saying as that's what the government thought. You see, up until lately the raw material for our success had mostly to come from out of the ground – and that made the miners powerful. It made them see they could get better pay, if only they could sort themselves out.

'And that's when the unions came along. They got the miners to band together and challenge what the government did. There's some as say it went too far, but that's another story. It brings us up to what's happening today: because what's going on is all about power, and the deliberate destruction of an industry by a government who don't want to be challenged again.'

Mr Brierly fell silent a minute, and Mick chewed at the side of his lip. He had the idea again, of things coming together like the pieces of a puzzle, and these things being reflected in his drawings.

Mr Brierly said, 'Do you know what I'm trying to tell you, Mick? Do you understand Mr Riley a bit better now? He didn't mean that the miners were fodder. He meant they were blokes with talent to spare – and that brings us nicely back to today – because some of that talent's rubbed off on to you!'

Inside Mick a fist was slowly unclenching.

He said, 'This picture's not to go up in the hall. It's for Grandpa to look at on his own. I'm doing his story for him to see and this is just a part of it. But I'll help the others with the paper coal.'

'Your grandpa's a lucky man, Mick Cotton.' Mr Brierly gave a cough to clear the air. Then he nodded at Mick's picture. 'I'm going to roll this up properly, and you're to collect it from me before you go home.' He grinned at Mick and gave him a push. 'So go on then, laddie – don't just stand there looking daft – get stuck into those lumps of coal!'

After school Mick went across to see Paul. Paul had not been at school that day, and Mick guessed it was because of the cold in his chest. But when he got to Paul's house there was no one in.

Mick waited for a while in the gathering rain, then shrugged and turned back down the path. He expected Paul was just bunking off.

When he got back home his mam was in and she was listening to the radio. Mick held his breath and waited a bit, but his mam did not start to join in with the tune, she carried on peeling potatoes.

So Grandpa had not had one of his turns. And his mam was behaving normally. Last night Mick told her he would be joining the band and his mam had given him a long, slow look. There was no expression on her face. All she said was, 'You will, will you?' and then she had gone back to reading her book.

Now Mick took the picture out of his bag and put it on the table.

'Look, Mam,' he said, 'I did this at school.'

His Mam put the potato peeler down and crossed over to the table. She looked at the picture with her head on one side. 'I can't make head nor tail of that.'

'It's the way you feel at the bottom of a mine!'

'I don't know what to make of you! The way you go and get your ideas! You know you can't go down the pit. Bilston'll be closed when you leave school.'

'This is Grandpa's story, Mam! It's about the things that happened to him. And any road – I don't want to go down mine – I want to be an artist instead!'

'You can't make a living out of doing that! You've to get yourself a proper job. You could go in for being a teacher, maybe. Or an accountant at one of them firms in town.'

The excitement of the picture had gone to Mick's head. All at once the future seemed blindingly, brilliantly, wonderfully clear: he would be an artist when he left school, because that was what he wanted to be! But how could he make his mam understand? He said slowly, 'You can turn yourself into whatever you like. It makes no difference if the pit is closing. You can be whatever you want to be.'

'You might think different when the time comes round.'

His mam turned back to the bowl of potatoes like she was stepping into a separate world. Mick stared at her back with the stiffness in it. He said, 'It can't be helped, Mam, the way I am. I reckon it's to do with nature.'

'Nature be blowed! It's from your dad – there's a touch of Irish in the Cotton line! Now let me get on with the spuds, will you? You'll need tea early if you're going out.'

Mick went back to the table to pick up his picture. The radio was playing a jaunty tune, and then the news came on: '*Today it was announced that Marston Pit is to close down with the loss of five hundred jobs. Marston Pit is one of the most efficient pits in the*

Midlands area. A spokesman said today, "We've done everything they asked us to do and nothing we do is good enough." Marston Pit was sunk in 1952. Its closure makes it the tenth pit to close in the last twelve months.

'More local news: thieves broke into a knitwear factory and stole the money from the overnight safe. Police estimate the amount to be about twenty thousand pounds. The security guard was coshed on the head, but is recovering in hospital.'

'I'm going upstairs to see Grandpa.'

'Right-oh, love. Your tea'll be ready in half an hour.'

But Grandpa was asleep when Mick went in. It was nearly dark outside, and Grandpa's room was full of shadows. Grandpa was lying on his back and his body made a very small lump under the bedclothes. Mick tiptoed round the end of the bed and Blu-tacked the picture on the wall. Grandpa would see it when he woke up and would know that Mick had put it there.

After tea Mick took the cornet from his cupboard. That morning he had played a loud B flat. The noise had echoed round the room like the trumpeting of an elephant. And then there had been the bang of a door, and footsteps clonking on the lino. His mam had come bursting into the room.

'You've just about given me a heart attack! I thought your grandpa was at it again!'

His mam's face was still swollen and flushed from sleep, and her nightie trailed at the hem.

'Sorry, our Mam. I didn't think.'

'That's your trouble, isn't it? You never seem to blooming well think! And do you know what time it is? It's only six o'clock! I've a full day's work ahead of me and I've got to get up in another hour!'

Mick's dad appeared behind his wife. 'Come on, Susie, love, let's get back to bed. You can have a bit-yell later.' There was a shadow of stubble on his chin and his hair was standing up in a crest. He gave Mick a wink over the top of her head, 'Put that thing away back in the cupboard, son – and then you'd better get your head back down!'

Now Mick put the cornet into his bag and went downstairs to the kitchen. His dad was washing up at the sink.

'I'm off out now, to Charlie Binns'.'

'Good luck then, son. Mind how you go.'

Mick hitched the bag up on to his shoulder and walked across to the door. He rarely saw his dad on his own. Sometimes Mick thought it was a bit like having a cheerful stranger to stay. If Mick was poorly or needed a clout, his mam was the one to see to it. His dad always joked and gave him sweets – but now there was something Mick wanted to know.

He cleared his throat and twitched at the bag. But he did not know how to talk to his dad. He hesitated another second or two, then said abruptly, 'Our Mam don't like that Charlie Binns!'

His dad squeezed the dishcloth out very thoroughly, and hung it to dry across the taps. He seemed to be thinking while he did it. Then he said to Mick, 'Oh, don't she, now? What made you suddenly come out with that?'

Mick shrugged his shoulders and looked at his feet. It was a stupid question for his dad to ask.

Mr Cotton dried his hands on the kitchen towel. 'You don't want to fret about your mam. She'll come round to Charlie in the end.'

And if that was not just like his dad! Mick stayed silent. His dad was not comfortable with real feelings, he liked folk to be happy all the time. Arguments and dissension made him uneasy, and sometimes it made him back away. But for now his dad seemed genuinely puzzled. He kept rubbing the side of his face with his hand, as if he was baffled as to what to say.

Mick examined the squares on the lino. He said, 'She don't like the mine and she don't like the band! She don't like anything much round here, and sometimes I think she don't like me!'

'Get off it, Mick, you're talking daft!' Mr Cotton leaned his back against the sink. 'It's rubbish to say your mam don't like you – I happen to know she likes you a lot! Only sometimes I think she feels a bit shut out. You see, her mam – and by that I mean your Grandma Brown – died when she was still quite young, and your mam started lacking for company. Your grandpa had his work and his mates and the band – he put his grief into all of that, and that's how it was for blokes just then. Your mam's frightened she'll lose you like she lost her pa – that's what she thinks when she sees you getting wrapped up with Charlie Binns and all his mates in the Bilston Band. You just have to try to be patient a bit – let her know she's not left behind.'

Mick stared at his dad. He was staggered to hear him come out with this! Mick wanted to make things right with him, but for once he was stuck for something to say.

And his dad seemed to know what *he* was thinking!

He came over and put an arm round Mick. 'You go and enjoy yourself at Charlie's. I'll square things up here with your mam.'

Mick went outside. The coldness of the rain helped to cool his hot face. He could not get over what had happened. Until now he had thought Bilston was a boring place, but just lately it was full of mystery and surprise. It was like turning the pages of a book and never knowing how it would end.

The Binns' house was on Chatsworth Terrace. There were two rows of houses facing each other across a narrow walkway. Charlie's house was as neat as a new pin. Snowflake curtains gleamed at the windows and the doorstep was scrubbed to a gleaming white.

Mick knocked self-consciously at the door, and it opened straight away.

'Eeh! Come in, Mick, love, we're expecting you.'

Mrs Binns took hold of his arm very firmly and dragged him into the hall. The inside of the house was as neat and shiny as the outside looked. It was like walking into a very plush cage. Mick's feet sank into a thick purple carpet; there were flowers in a brass pot at the foot of the stairs, and flowers rioted across the walls.

'Will you have a banana or a bacon sandwich? Or will you have a cup of tea?'

Mrs Binns was a bit like a flower herself; her dress was covered with large pink roses, and her face was shiny and pink and white. She smelled of bacon and lily of the valley. There was a warmth and cosiness in Charlie's house that made Mick feel as if he had just come home.

'No, ta, Mrs Binns. I've had me tea.'

'Come in the living-room by the fire.'

'Steady on, Muriel, he's come to see me!'

Charlie squeezed past his wife in the little hall. Then he opened the door to the best front room. The front room was colder than the hall. There was a leatherette settee against one wall, and an upright piano in a space near the window.

'Our Muriel's got an eye for the lads – don't let her get you alone in there!'

The way Charlie spoke made Mick relax. He liked the cosy stuffiness of the rooms. It was a bit like being in a foreign country where none of the stresses of home applied.

Charlie spread some music out on a stand. 'Now then, lad, get your instrument out. Let's see if you can play that note – have you had a bit of a blow today?'

'Aye – I did it this morning at the crack of dawn and nearly got me head smashed in!'

'Well, try it again. Don't forget what I said about your lips – just pretend you're blowing a tea leaf out.'

Mick took a deep breath and blew very hard. A rich brass sound came tumbling out.

'That's it! That's the one! Now what did I tell you that note was?'

'B flat, you said. That's the same note Grandpa played on his cornet.'

'Right, lad. And this is B flat on the music chart. Have a good look to see where it is, and then we'll do another note. We'll be playing "Slaidburn" when we go on the march and that's all top and bottom. I'll likely get you to play all the D's – but in the meantime I'm going to teach you five notes.'

It was amazing the way Charlie seemed to change the moment he had to do with the band. It was all wrapped up with what Grandpa said – about love being the thing that kept a band going. Love brought power and authority, but it was not the same power as the government.

'Now I want you to blow for me again, and this time we'll do another note. If you make your lips tight, you get a high note like this . . .' Charlie blew a note that made the pictures rattle on the walls. '. . . and if you make your lips slack you get a low note like this . . .' A sound like a cow lowing oozed into the room. Mick thought it was the loneliest, deep-blue sort of sound that he had ever heard.

'Now you have a go and think what I said.'

Mick breathed in deeply. Then he made his lips go as slack as he could, and blew out very hard. The noise that emerged was like a frog croaking: *croo-ak, croo-ak, croo-ak!*

'Don't be put off if you don't get it first time. Just try again and do your best, because that's what playing's all about.'

Croo-ak, croo-ak!

'And again!'

Croo-ak!

'And again.'

A sound like Sunday afternoon came out. A Sunday afternoon in summertime, with the peonies in bloom and the scent of tobacco floating up from old men's pipes.

'That's it, lad! You've cracked it! Now do it again – and when you've done that, do it some more!'

Mick's face was shiny and wet with sweat. He had never thought playing would be as hard as this, but it was hard work he thought he would enjoy. If Mick could draw the way the sound made him feel, he would draw a huge molten glow with a deep-blue heart.

'You're doing great, Mick! Now look-you here – this is the note you've been playing today. It's B – look where it is on the chart. See where it is in relation to B flat. Remember you had slack lips for that, and then just keep on practising! Next time you come we'll have a look at your fingers and see what we can make of them – what're you doing on Friday night?'

'Nothing much as I know of yet.'

'Then I'll see you round here again at six o'clock! Now – what do you say to a pint with the lads?'

Before Mick could answer, Mrs Binns shouted up, 'I heard that, Charlie Norman Binns! You're not to go leading that lad astray – he's not old enough yet to go to the pub. If he wants to, he can stay here with me.'

Charlie winked at Mick, and then cocked an eyebrow at the door. 'See what I told you?' he said in a loud whisper. 'My old lady's one for the boys!'

Mick set off home through the village. The stars were out, and over Hangman's Wood there was a thin winter moon. For a while Mick stood and stared at it. In a few years' time he would leave Bilston, he would leave it behind for good. But for now there was a magic to the place he had not ever noticed before. All the way up the village street there were little squares of orange light. Mick could name the people behind each door; there was a continuity about life in Bilston that would soon be shattered and gone for good.

Mick wanted to finish his grandpa's story, and he sensed the urgency in that. But as well as the story, there was something else: Mick was startled by the way the cornet made him feel – because now, more than ever, the thing he wanted most of all, was to carry on and play with the band.

7 Cowslip day

The axle bottoms were slick with grease, and there was grease on your hands you could never wash off. The grease seemed to suck and lap at your skin like some huge, great, slavering, hungry dog. It got in your nails, your hands went black, and even soap didn't wash it off, so your food didn't taste right after a while – not unless you liked the taste of the pit.

The way you coped was to watch yourself as if you were watching a stranger; you'd watch yourself bent over the carts while the real you just stood back and laughed. The real you was far away . . . he was tossing cowslips into a bucket, and the cowslips had the smell of spring . . . a golden, honeyed, new-grown smell, as if you had managed to catch the sun . . .

Mick did not know where the yellow came from, he thought maybe it was the light reflecting yellow on to the page. But his hand was clutching a thick yellow pencil and he was busily making yellow flowers. It was after midnight, and Mick was working by the light from his bedside lamp. He was trying not to rustle the paper in case his mam or dad woke up. They had caught him drawing once before and he had said he would not do it again – but he had not actually made a promise to them. It was telling what Mick called a soft sort of lie; it was a lie that did not do any harm; it was to make things better than they were, and at the same time to try and keep the peace.

The flowers were rampaging over the page in a glorious sprawl of yellow. It was as if they could sense the urgency of the thing that Mick was trying to do and they were almost drawing their own flower shapes.

But time was running out.

And now he was drawing yellow flowers when he wanted to draw the woman's face.

Everything in its proper time. One of Grandpa's sayings, that. It seemed to Mick that it was Grandpa emerging through the flowers and that was the thing that puzzled him: he may not be ready to draw the face – but what had Grandpa to do with flowers?

His mam was the one who would like the flowers – they were something you could almost smell – but they belonged to Grandpa in some mysterious way, and it was *his* face Mick could see coming through.

Mick put down the pencil and got into bed. Now that he had finished his drawing he was suddenly freezing cold. He tried to focus his mind back on the flowers to work out what they could possibly mean. But maybe he was tireder than he thought, because the yellow flowers became blurred in his mind, they twisted into weird shapes, grouping and regrouping, then forming into different patterns until they became a yellow cornet. Mick's feet were marching in time to the band, but whenever he put the cornet to his lips he saw Grandpa's face there instead of his own. It was as if he was marching inside a ghost, but it was not a ghost to scare folks with. It was a light-hearted, joyous sort of feeling, as if you were made of sunshine and air.

Mick thought he would go and see Grandpa in the morning and ask him about the yellow flowers. There was a lot of stuff he wanted to know, but in the meantime . . .

Mick slept.

. . . There was something Mick could not quite make out . . . something whirring away into distant space like a streak of yellow light. First a flash high in the sky, and then nothing, just a pale primrose after-glow. Mick was running along in the after-glow trying to find the yellow light, but his feet were somehow weighed down . . . he could not seem to move his feet . . .

'You're a bad lad, Mick! I shall say that now!'

Mick's mam was sitting on the side of the bed with a piece of paper clutched in her hand. The paper reflected yellow on her face, or else Mick thought his eyes were funny. Mrs Cotton was talking as if he was wide awake.

'You've been scribbling away at night again, and you promised me you wouldn't! What am I to make of you, I'd like to know? What am I to think if you carry on like this?'

There was frost outside the window again, and Mick's mam was dressed in her office clothes. The skirt she wore was as grey as the room and Mick saw that his bedside lamp was switched on. He tried to organise his thoughts into a sentence that would satisfy his mam.

'I didn't ever promise,' he said, 'I only sort of agreed with you.'

'You and your soft lies again! I'd like to get inside your head and give it a good clean sweep sometime!'

But Mrs Cotton only sounded cross. When Mick looked at her face it was softer than usual, as if she was really pleased about something but did not want to show it to Mick. She twitched at the piece of paper in her hand, and then held it up to the light. 'These flowers, our Mick,' she said, 'you've done 'em great – it's better than the stuff you usually do. If I close my eyes I can smell them now. You're a good lad to go doing this for me.'

Mick blinked.

'Yeah, well . . .'

The cowslips did not belong to his mam but he could not get them back! Not, at any rate, without hurting her feelings and Mick was not prepared to do that. His mam had Grandpa's past clutched in her hand and she was holding it up to the winter light.

'When you want to you can draw real good. I'll show this later to your dad. Now, go and get yourself washed and dressed – I won't have you going late to school.'

Mick would show the picture to Grandpa later on and then he would have to give it her back, but there would be a gap on the wall in Grandpa's room.

When he got downstairs the picture was propped up against a shelf on the dresser. The bright spring flowers made the kitchen look darker and more dismal than it usually did. Even his mam looked grey in the light. For the first time Mick noticed how tired she was. There were lines going down from her nose to her mouth that had not been there a year ago, and there was a grey patch down the back of her hair.

Mick spooned the cereal into his mouth.

Then suddenly, without knowing he was going to do it, he said, 'Do you mind too much about me and the band?'

His mam was shovelling things into her bag: keys, a comb, a packet of mints. She did not look up from what she was doing.

'Mind?' she said. 'Of course I mind! But I reckon I'm more or less used to it now.'

'Well then . . .' It wasn't what Mick had wanted to hear, so he shrugged his shoulders and stayed quiet for a bit. His dad had gone out at the crack of dawn, and there was not much noise apart from the radio and the clatter of Mick's spoon against the dish. Over the top of it he could hear his mam muttering to herself: 'Toothpaste, soap, peas and spuds . . .' Then all at once she stopped her muttering. She went very still and said, 'Mick, look at me, will you? You asked if I minded about the band. Well of course I *mind* about it – I'd rather you didn't go in for it, but if that's what you really want to do, you must get right on and do it. I just didn't want it all over again. I expected you'd be different to that.'

'It's just a band, Mam! It's just something I want to do now! I don't want it for good and all – and any road up, I'll be away from Bilston in a year or two . . .'

Mick stopped himself and swallowed hard. The idea of leaving Bilston had crystallised into a definite plan. He would leave Bilston and go to college, but he had not yet told his mam about that!

He waited for her to say something. She said, 'Aye, well, we'll see about that. Just say ta-ra to your grandpa for me.'

But Grandpa was sleeping when Mick went upstairs. As the days went by he was sleeping more and more. And there was less of him now than there used to be. His body was getting thinner and thinner like a waning moon, but the real Grandpa was still inside; the same awkward cuss, the cock o'the walk; the bloke who was always one up on his mates.

When Mick got to school there was no sign of Paul. His desk was tidy and his coat was not there. Everything looked very neat and clean, but for some reason Mick felt slightly scared – and he had learned to trust his feelings; if he tried to ignore them they just got worse.

At lunch-time he went over to Paul's. The frost had melted and the sun was out, but it felt odd to be there in the middle of the day, as if he was playing hooky from school.

Mick stood outside the iron fence and peered at Paul's house through the garden. Now that he was here there was a churning sensation in the pit of his stomach; his head was buzzing and he could not breathe.

The house looked strangely flat in the sunshine, as if all the angles had been smoothed away. The water in the tub at the side of the door was flat and opaque and very still. There was no sign of Paul, and the curtains at the upstairs windows were drawn.

Mick did not want to go down the path. He did not want to be drawn towards the strange, flat stillness of the house. There was an idea in his head that if he ventured any further he would be sucked into some terrible secret and that in the end he would be sorry. Then the door opened and Paul came out. He stood on the step with his hands in his pockets, just looking around and sniffing the air. He looked different, and the clothes he was wearing were brand spanking new.

Mick knew Paul's clothes like he knew his own. They were a motley collection of moth-eaten jeans and manky shirts, and coats inherited from his dad. But these clothes were bright and crisp and new. The jeans had that stiff, not-yet-washed look about them, and the jumper was thick and heavy with stripes across it in red and blue.

Without thinking, Mick called out softly, 'Paul! Quick! Over here!'

He stayed crouched down low behind the fence so that Paul had to follow the sound of his voice.

'Paul – come on, mate – over here!'

Paul came down the path very slowly. He kept looking back at the house and the curtained upstairs window. The way he looked made Mick think that he was scared of something; that something was wrong inside Paul's house.

Paul was walking along with his hands in his pockets and his shoulders very stiff.

'How are you then, mate?'

Paul shrugged at him and kicked at a stone. He looked like a stranger in his stiff new clothes, as if he was wearing a skin too many, and the skin did not quite fit.

'OK I s'ppose. What's up with you?'

'Nowt as usual. You coming to school?'

Paul kicked at the fence and bits of rust went floating down. His jeans made a starchy, crackling noise whenever he moved, but he still wore the same scuffed black shoes.

'Dunno,' he said. 'Things are funny for us just now. Me dad got bonked on the head in the raid. You probably heard it on the news. He's laid up in bed and me mam's dead worried – she's keeping me off for company, like.'

Mick knew Paul's dad had given up on the mines. He worked as a guard in a place up town and he wore a blue tunic with a smart peaked cap. He went off to his job at night, and Mick had seen him once from his bedroom window, crossing the road like a navy blue ghost.

'Go on! You're joking! Company? You?'

'You can cut the cackle or I'll belt you one! I'm telling you – that's what she said.'

Mick gave a loud crack of laughter. He wanted Paul to come through the fence, though he could not rightly understand why. He said, 'Come on out here and belt me then! Yer mam must be daft if she wants you at home!'

Paul pushed his way through the scruffy fence. Flakes of rust were clinging to his jumper and the hems of his jeans were sopping wet. But he was grinning at Mick and flailing his fists.

'Who's got muck on his fancy pants?'

Paul tucked his head down into his shoulder and then rushed at Mick so they both fell down. Where the frost had melted, the earth was thick and dark like black clotted cream. Mick could smell the winter blackness of the soil, all mixed in with the smell of new clothes.

'Ow – get off! What's really to-do?'

Mick could hear the cold air whistle through his chest, and the fight had brought Paul's cough back on.

'Me dad's got one of his tempers again. I reckon it was the knock on his head as did it. He won't go out and he keeps shouting at Mam.'

Mick's guts were tightening up again. He had a vision of Mr Reeve caged like a lion, roaring his head off and rattling at the bars.

'You can come down home with me if you like.'

'Naah. I got me mam to think of now. Besides, our dad'll be better soon.'

They got to their feet and dusted themselves down. Mick felt both better and worse at the same time. Without Paul he was lonelier than he thought . . . and apart from Paul there was Mr Reeve. Mick knew immediately that something was wrong; something he did not understand; something secret and deeply disturbing – and maybe something even Paul did not know.

Mick's gift was a blessing and a curse to him – because what was the use of sensing danger if you could not prevent a thing taking place?

His head was starting to ache again.

'See you soon, then, shall I, mate?'

Paul shrugged his shoulders. 'Aye, maybe.'

Mick turned round to go at the same time as they heard the back door creak open. They glanced at each other and looked away.

'Paul!' His mam was shouting from the step. 'Where are you, Paul? Come on back here, I want you in.'

Mrs Reeve's voice was usually quite hoarse and low – mainly, Paul said, because of all the cigarettes. But today her voice sounded high and thin.

Paul nodded at Mick, 'See you then, mate,' and scrambled back through the scruffy fence. A few seconds later a door slammed shut and Mick slowly made his way back to school.

The class were busy with their bit of the mural. It showed a pit-pony being led along by a grinning miner in a hard orange hat. The picture was a riot of colour and movement, as if the pit was not really dark and the sun was somewhere close at hand. The dirt on the faces looked terribly clean, and the pony's legs were too long and thin.

Mick found that he enjoyed disapproving of the mural. It made him feel a bit superior, as if he knew something different to the other kids, but was not going to tell.

'Are you with us today, or shall I send you a letter?'

Miss Watson's shadow was across his desk. Miss Watson was dressed in her arty clothes: a long black smock and thick black tights, with her hair done up in a wispy bun. There was a piece of paper in her hand and she plonked it down in front of Mick.

'If you're not going to do your bit with the mural, you might as well get on with this. You're to do it in your best handwriting – and mind you don't go spilling the ink.'

The paper was a list of events and statistics all to do with Bilston Pit: forty per cent on free school dinners, 500 laid off in one black week. The list went on and on, like a memorial to the living dead. Writing it down seemed to bring it home: Bilston depended on the pit, there was nothing left once it had gone.

When school was over Mick stamped on home. He wanted to spend the night in front of the telly and watch all the rubbishy comedy shows. And maybe he would drink a glass of beer . . . The evening Mick had spent with Grandpa and his mates came seeping back into his skull. He forgot the bit about being sick and remembered the lovely floaty feeling; voices eddying through the dark and the way the world was slowly shut out.

He let himself in through the blue front door and slung his bag down on the mat. There was a radio playing close at hand and at first his brain did not register the fact. A man was singing 'If I Ruled the World' and someone was singing along with it. His mam was supposed to be at work – but what if his grandpa was taken bad? The doctor's car was not parked outside – but what if Grandpa had been carted away?

Mick found that his legs were heavy again, and his hands were clenched into two tight fists. He made himself walk to the living-room door, and he pushed it open to a blaze of light. Grandpa was sitting in the big armchair; he was wheezing along to the stupid tune and beating time with his hands.

'Grandpa, you bogger! You scared me stiff! I heard the music through the door and I thought as how you must have been took!'

'You thought it was your mam in here! You thought it was our Sue, singing along the way she does when she's thinking to try and shut me out!'

'Aye, I did if you really want to know – and look what you've done to the arm of that chair. When Mam comes home she'll skin you alive!'

There was a puddle of beer on the arm of the chair with a ring of ash ground in it. Grandpa banged on the pink plush arm with his fist. 'I'm still a man in me own blooming house!'

'But this is Mam's house you live in, Grandpa. You came over to live with us when you was first took bad!'

Grandpa stopped his banging. He seemed surprised by what Mick said. His mouth opened a bit then closed again, as if he was thinking things over. Finally he gave a sigh. 'Aye, lad,' he said, 'you're right about that: I reckon you're right about most things now, so mebbe, I should think, you're right about this.'

Grandpa was forgetting things, and it might have been the effect of the beer. These days he did not eat very much, so there would be nothing inside him to sop it up. Grandpa picked at his food to keep his daughter quiet; 'She goes on at me to eat my greens as if I'm a lad and not her dad!' and the beer most likely had gone to his head.

But there was nothing more that Mick could say for fear of making him mad again.

And Grandpa was glancing sharply at Mick. He said, 'I seen the picture you done up there.'

The yellow flowers were on the shelf. They created their own bright pool of light, so you could feel your eyes being drawn to them wherever you were standing in the room.

'I decided to give them to our Mam. She took a fancy to them straight away.'

'Aye, she would do, lad. She was always a sucker for flowers, your mam. She used to cry her heart out on cowslip day – and that was before you was even born, when your mam was just a nipper. She'd sit behind the hedge with her face in her hands and she'd sob as if there was no tomorrow. She'd a soft heart on her, had your mam – still has, I daresay, though she hides it well. She couldn't stand to see the flowers ripped up like they were and tossed in the buckets just any old how. She thought we were killing them and they'd never come back – and in a way she was right about that. You hardly ever see a cowslip now.'

'You what?' Mick was confused. The cowslips had come of their own accord, and he had assumed they were to do with Grandpa. But out of the blue his mam had cropped up – and what had she to do with it all?

Grandpa said, 'The first Sunday in May was cowslip day. Folks'ud come from the city and pick the cowslips to take away and sell up the town. They'd come out here any way they could – on bikes, in carts and cars and on foot. They'd wind the stems with bits o'twine and sell 'em in bunches for a few pence apiece, and what they didn't sell got made into wine, and cowslip wine was like liquid spring. They'd draft extra police in to deal with the blokes – because Sunday or not, the pubs'd be open all day long – we'd be washing them out of the bar at midnight and there'd be all manner of shenanigans going on. But it were a way of making a bob or two and I did a bit of picking myself. You never thought the cowslips'd ever run out, you just took it for granted they'd always be there. I'd roll in cowslips on me back and feel like I was rolling in the sun.'

Mick stroked the picture with his hand. The yellow seemed to come off the page; it felt warm and silky to the touch.

'I'll do another picture if you like.'

Grandpa smoothed his hair with the flat of his hand. 'No lad,' he said after a time, 'them flowers rightly belong to your mam. She's earned 'em, I reckon, if anyone has. Now then – are you going to give me a hand up them stairs? I'm dicky on my pins just now – drunk again as yer mam'll say – and mighty happy it makes me too!'

Mick put his arm round Grandpa's waist. He was amazed at how thin and light he was – and he had thought of his grandpa as such a big man!

Later that night Mick lay in bed. It was cold enough to freeze your toes and if the light was on you could see your breath. But he could smell the flowers. It was springtime and the sun was out. Cowslips were out at the top of Hobbs field, and below it the march was going by.

But time was marching as fast as the band. Mick was scared when he thought how fast it went. And Grandpa was clearly weaker now. Would he still be here when the pit closed down?

Would he actually see Mick march with the band?

8 Tin Lurky

He could smell the cake his mam had baked, and she'd tried to make it one of her best. It was a big golden dome stuffed full of currants with sugary bits stuck down the sides. She smiled at him when she cut the first slice, 'Sixteen,' she said, 'you're nearly a man.' Tomorrow was the day he was to go on the face, because that's what happened when you got to sixteen. It was a way of proving you were fully grown – the face was what made you into a man.

But his insides were twisted into knots; he kept imagining the roof come roaring in. Sweat was gleaming on dead men's faces and his knees were beat from being bent so long. The band was the thing that kept him going: the sweet blue notes drowned out the pit. If he closed his eyes he could make himself hear 'Liberty Bell', 'Kenilworth', the 'Chieftain', and the 'Standard of Saint George' . . .

'You're handless, Mick Cotton! What are you?'

'Handless, Mr Binns.'

'That's right! That's what you are! Now can you count to three, or is it asking too much? I want *three* fingers on the valves, d'you see? Not the whole flaming bunch of fives!'

Mick was standing with Charlie in the little front room and he could not get the fingering right. To his shame he found he could not read music and blow and depress the valves all at the same time. And the more Charlie shouted, the worse it became: his hands slithered over the gleaming brass; the notes he blew sounded flat in his ears, like a foghorn on a murky night.

'Come on then, lad, let's try again – and give it a bit of thought this time. You're to play D, E and F for me, right? And don't forget about your lips.'

A trickle of sweat ran down Mick's ribs. There was no fire on in Charlie's front room, but the windows were steamed up and running with wet. Mick thought if he stayed in the room much longer he would vaporise into a puddle of water on the floor and have to be carried out in a bucket.

He grinned at the thought without knowing he was doing it, and wiped his hands on the seat of his pants.

'That's right, lad, grin if you want to – you're not leaving this room until you've got those notes!'

Charlie was trying his best to make Mick play, but somehow that only made things worse. Mick could not make his hands connect with his brain, and he had always thought he was good with his hands. He could hear the notes he wanted to play, but he could not translate the idea of music into physical effort with his fingers and lips.

And Charlie Binns was shouting again!

'Think of the notes as three, two, one if it'll make it easier for you to grasp. That has a rhythm all of its own – it sounds more natural than D, E, F.'

Mick closed his eyes and blew a note; but the noise that came out was like a balloon going down. There was a rumbling hiss with a gasp at the end, and then nothing but the hiss of the rain outside.

He gave a long, deep, despairing sigh.

'What's the matter with you, lad? Have you lost your puff?'

And then a question slipped out without Mick thinking. He said to Charlie, 'Did Grandpa have a job like me? Or did it come to him more natural, like?'

Charlie darted Mick a quick, sharp look. Then he leaned against the mantelpiece and folded his arms across his chest.

'Your grandpa was a bit before my time when he was starting off. But I heard as how he blew so sweet and true it made your toes curl in your socks. He had a feel for brass, did Gilbert Brown. He didn't just blow for sommat to do: his heart and soul went into that brass.'

Mick looked down at the carpet with its swirly pattern of pink and mauve. He imagined Grandpa painting pictures with music; the whole of his life played out in brass.

He glanced at Charlie, then looked away.

'I can't seem to get the hang of music.'

'And Gil couldn't paint to save his life! You can't have all the talents, me lad – you just have to try a bit harder with some.'

Mick opened his mouth to make a reply, but before he could speak a voice called out: 'Charlie Binns! I'll not have you working that lad too hard – he's to have some puff left over for me!'

Charlie gave a jump, then winked at Mick. 'Quick before the missus comes – give it your best just one more time before she comes and wallops me over the head!'

D, E, F. 3, 2, 1. Mick blew three notes in a row without stopping. The notes were wobbly and a bit fuzzy round the edges, but they were still a lot better than the balloon going down.

'You're getting there, son, but you've to practise more than most. I expect as how Gil would help you out if you were to ask him nicely when you got home.'

Mick turned away without bothering to answer. He made a business out of carefully wrapping the cornet up in a clean, soft, linen cloth. The truth was he would never dare to ask Grandpa for help; for some reason the idea of it made him feel shy. He thought it would be a bit like painting with numbers, as if he was belittling what Grandpa had done. Mick wanted to emerge from Charlie's hands as a good, clean player – a player good enough to march with the band. But he wanted to do it without Grandpa's help, and that was a thing he could not explain.

Charlie was packing his music away in a worn leather case. Now that the lesson was over he seemed oddly deflated, not so much in size, but in noise and volume, as if the lesson had taken as much out of him as it had out of Mick.

He snapped the case shut and said to Mick, 'You'd better come down the pub with me, or you'll finish up holding Muriel's wool.'

And if he went to the pub Mick's mam would know, and it was likely she'd kill him with one of her looks! Mick could not decide the best thing to do.

In the end he said, 'I'll just come with you for half an hour – me mam'll kick up, like, if I'm late getting home.'

'They take some sorting, these womenfolk do!'

Charlie was shrugging himself into a big, brown overcoat. He had a brown woolly scarf tied round his neck. To Mick it made him look like a fat, brown, grizzly bear. He pulled open the front door and a spatter of rain blew into the hall.

'You're taking me boyfriend away again – you thought I wouldn't know what you're at!'

Charlie's wife surged into the hall. She caught hold of Mick and gave him a hug. It was like being hugged by a big, squashy cushion; there was the scent of lily of the valley again, and a hint of the onions she had cooked for tea.

'Behave yourself, Muriel! Let the lad go – he'll be getting the wrong idea about us!'

Muriel planted a kiss on the side of Mick's face, and in spite of himself he started to blush. His mam would never behave like that! In their family they did not go in for much kissing – he had not kissed his mam since he was a kid, and he was sure as he could be she had never kissed him. You only got touched in the Cotton house if you were laid up poorly with something in bed, and then a hand might be stroked across your forehead to try and see how hot it was. The way Muriel hugged him made Mick feel pleased and embarrassed both at the same time. He fancied giving her a quick hug back, but his arms stayed stiff against his sides.

'There now, I've been and gone and embarrassed the lad!' Muriel gave his cheek a swift, sharp pinch and then pushed him off towards the front door. 'Look after Charlie, will you, me duck? He's not to have more than a couple of pints!'

The pub they went to was the Dog and Duck, and Mick had been there once before with Paul. They had sat on a seat going red in the face, feeling scared they would get clocked as under-age and the barman would come and chuck them out.

Going there with Charlie was different to that; it was proof of sorts that he was growing up. It was one of the things you did in Bilston: it was a way of becoming one of the blokes.

But supposing he went and got it wrong?

Mick glanced at Charlie uncertainly. He did not know what he would say to the men whose faces he could make out behind the smoke.

'What'll you have, son – a double rum?'

'Half a bitter, please.'

Charlie grinned at him and tapped his nose. 'Better make it a shandy, Mick me lad – can't have you getting legless again or I'll have your mam running after me!'

Whenever Charlie spoke about women he made it sound as if they were a race apart – as if they were the huge, fierce creatures from seaside postcards and cartoon strips. Charlie's women fairly bristled

87

with curlers and rolling-pins, and yet Mick could sense his contentment with Muriel.

'Park theeself over here, Mick lad!'

There was a space made for him at a wooden bench and Mick sat with his back against the wall.

'So how's old Gil, then? Going on all right?'

'He's still very poorly, Mr Beale.'

'Call me Will, like everyone else. It's rough on old Gil, I'll tell you that. The best are always the first to go.'

'I'll second that!'

Mick's eyes were starting to smart and sting from the smoke that was hanging in the room. For some reason he did not want to talk about Grandpa.

Then out of the blue he suddenly said, 'Well, I'll tell you sommat about our Grandpa, and that's for sure – he ain't dead yet!'

There was a sudden hush around the table. The words Mick had spoken seemed to hover in the air, echoing and spreading through the thick blue smoke. Then, very slowly and deliberately, Mr Beale put his glass down on the table. He said to Mick, 'Aye, young man. You're right about that.'

People began chatting to each other again, and the evening seemed to melt away into a soft blur of beer and smoke, shot through with conversation.

'I could go to Yarmouth for under five quid. There'd be fifty shillings to get me there, a week's board and lodging and sommat to spend, and I'd still come back with half a quid.'

'You allus were a tight one, Ned.'

'. . . I don't wash me feet in case they go bad . . .'

'The unions used to be voluntary, but then they started to dock your pay . . .'

It was past nine o'clock when Mick got home. The rain had stopped, but the stars were hidden under a thick sheet of cloud.

His mam was in the living-room, watching the news on the television. The back of her neck was very stiff and straight. Without turning round she said to Mick, 'You reek of the pub. I daresay you went with that Charlie Binns.'

'I only had a shandy, Mam.'

'It's not what you've had, it's where you've *been*.'

His mam made it sound as if he had deliberately done something wicked and depraved. Mick looked at her back with the stiffness in it. He had a sudden flash picture of a girl with her face hidden inside her hands. The picture bothered and confused him; he only knew the Mam in the room. The girl she had been was someone he had never met.

He waited a while, and then went upstairs. Grandpa was asleep on his back and the room was full of the sound of his breathing. Through a gap in the curtains Mick could see the clouds parting slightly over the pit, and suddenly, for one brief, fierce moment he was glad that finally it was going to close down.

Mick went to his room and put the cornet down on the table. Tomorrow he would practise really hard, somewhere private like down the canal. Then he would go on the march in Grandpa's place if it was the last flaming thing he ever did!

Mick woke next day at the crack of dawn. The sky was faintly flushed with pink and somewhere a bird was starting to sing.

He picked up his pencil and began to draw. Jagged lines speared the page with an urgency that was frightening, and at the same time, terribly real. It was as if he was drawing something that he had experienced himself and not something he had seen in a dream. There was a tangle of fists and angry faces; a confusion of arms and legs and staves; a seething mass of collective hate.

By the time the drawing was completely finished, daylight was touching the room. The light made long, thin slivers of silver and white; it seemed to strike through the figures Mick had drawn like the flash of an assassin's knife, and Mick stared at the picture in his hand.

Who *were* these people? What were they to him? Not even Mr Reeve with his terrible temper had the same inflexible look of hate.

Mick went back to bed and tried to sleep, but his head was full of noise and movement, as if a battle was raging inside his skull. The picture must be to do with Grandpa – and yet Mick did not want to show it to him. There was an idea in his head that Grandpa was too frail now to deal with violence as stark as this. What if it brought back some terrible trauma? What if Mick was to blame for his death?

In the end Mick got out of bed. He pulled his clothes on and went downstairs. For some reason he did not want to go to school. What he wanted was a day that was free just for once, and so after a think he went round to Paul's.

Paul's bedroom was at the front of the house, which was lucky because it was away from his dog. Mick looked up at the window. The curtains did not quite meet in the middle and one of the windows was not properly shut. The front of the house was as messy as the back, with pieces of old car left lying about and a tarpaulin flapping against the hedge.

Mick picked up a handful of tiny pebbles and began to hurl them at Paul's window. At the fourth attempt Paul's face appeared like a flat white disc behind the mucky glass. He opened the window as wide as he could and leaned out over the sill.

'Wotcher want?' he asked in a loud whisper.

'I fancy a bit of company, like – d'you want to do Tin Lurky?'

Paul hesitated for a moment and looked up and down the scruffy road. He seemed to be thinking about something very hard, and that was unusual for Paul. But there was nothing to see, and no sound apart from a milk-float whirring along a couple of streets away.

Finally he said, 'OK then, mate, you're on. I'll be with you in a couple of secs.'

His head vanished from the window, and Mick put his hands in his pockets and leaned against the fence. Everywhere he looked there were signs of neglect; nothing was smart and properly cared for the way it always used to be.

Paul came outside wearing his oldest clothes: an ex-army pullover that had belonged to his dad and some green swirly trousers tied up with string.

They set off down the road without bothering to speak; past the houses on Railway Terrace, down Chatsworth Terrace and along the track to Hangman's Wood.

The track leading up to the wood was bounded on both sides by open land; scrubby meadows and unfenced fields and bands of scruffy Scots pines. They stopped out of sight of the last of the houses and Paul fished in his pocket and took out a penny.

'Toss you for Lurky,' he said to Mick. 'Heads you lose, tails I win!'

He spun the coin into the air and it landed on a patch of grass.

'Tails!' he said. 'You come after me, but you have to give me five minutes' start.'

Mick shrugged his shoulders and glanced at his watch. 'Half-past eight,' he said, squinting at it against the sun. 'Five minutes, you said – you'd better get going if you want a good run.'

Paul grinned at him and ran off down the path. The sun was higher than it had been for ages and the sky was a soft, milky white. It looked as though the day would be one of those fine, clear days you sometimes get in winter: what Grandpa would call a false blooming spring.

Mick jogged up and down a bit on the spot and then scanned the track further up ahead. Paul had vanished somewhere near the band of trees; there was no other living creature in sight, not even a rabbit scuttling about, or a bird on the grass, digging for worms.

Now that he was free of the village Mick felt one of those sudden, fierce jolts of happiness.

'*Yaa-hoo!*'

Mick yelled as loud as he could and Paul yelled back. He set off running up the track; the way Paul yelled he was *outside* the woods, over towards Black Bottom Pond. Mick stopped for a moment and took off his jacket. Sweat was trickling down his ribs and there was a stitch beginning in his side.

Paul was round a bend out of sight of the village. He was not making any attempt to hide.

'Lurky! Gotcher!'

'Lurky yourself!'

Paul's clothes lay in a heap beside the pond.

'What're you doing?'

'What do you think?'

'You're off your rocker – it's freezing in there!'

'Yer chicken, Mick Cotton – clu-ck, clu-ck, clu-ck!'

Paul flapped his elbows to try and keep warm.

'Come on if you're coming – don't stand there dithering like a big, soft girl!'

All at once Mick made up his mind. He struggled out of his heavy clothes and flung them down on the track. Without them he felt like a garden slug; he had not realised up until then, how small and vulnerable and pale he was.

Paul was waiting for him at a dip in the ground.

'One, two, three . . . *jump!*'

'A-argh!'

'Hell's flaming bells . . .'

'. . . and buckets of blood!'

Mick grabbed his clothes and rubbed them over his arms and

93

chest. Where the water had been there was a thin film of mud that had dried to a fine white tilth. His teeth were chattering and he could not stand still, but the shock of the water had cleared his head.

Suddenly he was filled with a blinding joy. It was like being present at the dawn of time. He wanted to stay where he was for ever and ever. He did not want to have to think about Grandpa. He did not want to return to school . . . and now, especially, he did not want to have to go home.

Mick's mam said, 'I don't know what to say to you. I don't know why you did what you did. You upset me, our Mick. I can't believe you went missing all day without so much as leaving a note. Now will you look at me when I'm speaking to you? I'm trying to tell you – I don't *understand.*'

It was teatime when Mick got back from the woods, and his mam was already waiting at home. She had not actually been to work, she had spent the day fretting about where he was.

'I'm sorry, Mam. I couldn't get myself off to sleep so I went out early and got carried away. I didn't think to leave a note.'

'You didn't think! You never do! That's half your trouble, if you was to ask me! You should spend more time having a good old think and a bit less time with a pencil in your hand.'

Mick's mam had been crying.

He stared down at his feet in their muddy shoes. His dad was out on a last-minute job, and there was nothing Mick could think of to say that would stop his mam from being angry and hurt. The magic of the day was gone, and all the old problems came surging back in.

'I'll not do it again. It were just this once.'

'And I suppose I shall have to write you a note. I shall have to tell them the truth at school.'

Mick shrugged his shoulders and made his face blank. School seemed to him like a huge waste of time. He edged his way towards the kitchen door.

'And don't think you can go up bothering Pa!'

'OK, I won't.' Mick made a movement with his hands, 'I'm sorry, Mam. I really am. I don't know what else you want me to say.'

Mick felt confused with the way things were: he did not want to upset his mam, but at the same time he was changing fast. He was changing into someone complicated; someone who wanted to play with the band because that was what he had promised Grandpa; and someone as well, who wanted to draw, who wanted to make his mam pleased and proud of this strange new person he had become.

His mam did not bother to make a reply and the kitchen was very dark and still. Mick had a sudden flash picture of Muriel; the opulent floweriness of her house, and the cushiony softness of one of her hugs. He waited to see if his mam would speak, but she hunched her shoulders and turned away.

He waited a bit longer, then left the room.

9 The strike

*If you forgot your tea you could die of thirst: blokes'd never give their
tea away. They needed it to put back the sweat that got lost when they
worked a shift on the face. Tea was the thing that kept him going . . .
tea and the rhythm he tried to set up to keep his mind busy and shut
out the fright. It was a fear that refused to go away and it made him
believe he was not a real man. Real men were not frightened of deep
dark places, only the mammy's boys admitted to that. But fear made
the sweat stand out on his skin; it made the breath catch tight in his
chest so he'd listen to himself and the noise he made, wheezing away
like a sick old dog.*

*And sometimes he'd catch the edge of a thought that added
another twist to his fear. The thought was nearly always the same . . .
'What if this is all there is? What if there's nothing more to life than
this grafting away in the dust and dirt?'*

Mick found that if he did not try to think too much it was usually
easier to get through the day. He tried to make his days fall into a

pattern of school and homework and practising the cornet down by the canal.

The canal had a kind of used-up emptiness; a decaying grandeur that exactly matched the frame of his mind. When he played a note the opaque stillness of the water seemed to lap it up and carry it away. Hardly anybody used the towpath now, just a fisherman some- times under a green umbrella, or an old bloke cycling home from work.

School was lately just a way to fill in time – but the trouble with school was: Paul was not there. His desk had been vacant for over a week and it was weird the way nobody mentioned him. Except for the register being called it was as if Paul had somehow ceased to exist; as if Mr Reeve's rage had swallowed him up, or he had fallen into a deep black hole. Only Mick seemed to think about him now, and the thinking made his bones start to ache. Something was wrong, Mick was sure of it, but he did not want to go to Paul's house. He was afraid if he did he might make things worse; that his own anxious fretting might upset Paul.

Every morning now when Mick woke up his mind was a jumble of impressions and thoughts. And the more he tried to make his mind a blank, the more the pictures seemed to come. There were the men with their hate looks and wooden staves; there was a bloke on his hands and knees in the dark. There was so much darkness and fear and hate ... and there was the woman he had seen at the main pit gate.

The woman Mick drew had a frightened face. Her bones were etched clearly under a translucent skin, and her eyes were huge and dark. The eyes were the thing that bothered Mick most. They were full of a sort of questioning terror that at heart knew what was really to-do. It was as if everything in Mick's life was heading inexorably towards disaster: Grandpa, Paul and the woman at the gate. Even when he was not in the room her eyes had the ability to follow him around. The woman looked at and through and beyond him, as if he had drawn a familiar ghost. Who was she?

Mick thought she was a part of Grandpa's story, that she was trying to tell him something important but had somehow managed to arrive out of turn.

He was trying to get the pictures into some kind of order, but it was a difficult job without Grandpa's help – and Grandpa was becoming frailer day by day. Mick was scared that the pictures would make him ill. But in the end he decided it was a risk he would take. He would show Grandpa most of the pictures he had drawn, but he would keep the picture of the woman back. Very carefully Mick put her away in a drawer with a mound of tissue paper on top.

When he got to Grandpa's room, Grandpa was out of bed. He was sitting in an armchair by the window with a tartan rug across his knees.

Grandpa said, 'So you've decided to come and see me at last?' And then he tucked his head down into his chest and folded his lips together.

Mick thought that he looked like a vulture; his shoulders were two wings sticking up on either side of his head and his nose was a beak poking out in the middle.

'I've been busy, Grandpa,' Mick said, 'so don't go looking at me like that. There's been a few things I wanted to do.'

Grandpa shot him a look that was full of venom. 'Aye!' he said. 'Busy making trouble, I hear! Busy upsetting your mam and dad!'

'Pack it in, Grandpa, will you? I've had enough without you carrying on – so d'you want me to stay up here or not?'

'You must please yourself, like you always do!'

Grandpa was mean and thin with rage – but not, Mick thought, with rage at him. It came to him that grandpa was tired of being weak and ill. Inside him was a massive bundle of energy that could not find a way of breaking free.

Mick said, 'Leave it off, Grandpa, will you? You know I come because I want to do . . .'

'Aye – and because you've got nowt else to do!'

Mick grinned to himself. In some peculiar kind of way Grandpa's rage was making *him* feel better – because, so long as Grandpa was making trouble, there was nothing much the matter with him.

Grandpa snorted suddenly, and untucked his chin from his chest. 'Well, lad,' he said, 'what have you got to show me, now as you've deigned to come up here?'

Mick unrolled a drawing and smoothed it out. The drawing showed a miner on his hands and knees and the miner was smiling into the dark – except that it was more a horrible baring of the teeth, and if you took the picture by surprise it turned from a smile into a grimace of fear.

Mick held the picture in his hands. Looking at it in Grandpa's room made him suddenly uncertain again.

'You won't like it, Grandpa,' he said, 'I'm warning you now, so don't blame me.'

He put the picture on the tartan rug and Grandpa fumbled about for his spectacles and put them on the end of his nose. He looked at the picture for a long, silent time, and then touched the man gently with the tip of his finger. He said slowly, 'You knock me for six some-times, young Mick, when you up and come out with stuff like this.'

'Were you very scared down there in the dark?' Mick found he could ask the question quite naturally, without having to take the time to think.

And Grandpa went very still and quiet. He seemed to be thinking deeply, and all the time he was doing his thinking he was brushing his finger to and fro against the man who was caught on the page.

Finally he said, 'Aye, lad, I was. I'll tell you now. I was more scared than you will ever know. I had that thing they've a name for now that makes you hate to be shut up. But I *had* to go down the mine, d'you see? There was nowt else for it. In them days you had to master your fears or you'd end up as the laughing-stock, and I'd rather be dead than have that shame.'

All his life Grandpa had been full of fear and Mick had never known it! Listening to Grandpa was like listening to an echo of himself. All that he was seemed to come from Grandpa, as if there was an invisible link between them. Mick discovered that he was staring at Grandpa without knowing he was doing it. He pulled his gaze back to the pictures and placed another one on Grandpa's knee.

He said, 'I nearly didn't show you this because I had the idea it would make you mad, and then our Mam'd be after me.'

The picture was the one of the men with the staves, and as soon as Mick uncovered it he had the same fierce jolt of shock and fear he had felt when he first completed it. Now when he looked at it, the figures seemed to shift on the page, as if the force of their own implacable hate impelled them along willy-nilly.

Grandpa glanced at the picture, and the muscles in his face went fine and taut.

'By gum you know how to get me going!'

His colour came up until his skin was as red as the tartan squares on the rug. He slapped at the picture violently.

'Have you been doing this at school or was there a programme on the telly?'

'It were neither, Grandpa, I don't work like that! I just draw the pictures as they come along.'

'And this is one I could do without! It's sommat as I thought I'd not see again.'

Grandpa looked bigger and stronger suddenly; more powerful and in control. Mick had the definite idea that in spite of his rage Grandpa was in some way actually enjoying himself. The picture seemed to trigger off a rush of excitement that made him forget for a moment how ill he was and start punching the air with his fists.

Grandpa said, 'What you've got here, lad is a bit of the strike, and maybe that was before your time. We were fighting these men to get into work. They came from further up north than here – they were Scargill's men and they did his dirty work.'

Grandpa was talking as fast as he could and gasping in between the words. His chest was moving up and down, and without being asked Mick fetched him the mask.

Grandpa breathed in very deeply. To Mick it seemed to take longer than usual to get Grandpa right. He found that he was breathing very slowly himself in time to Grandpa's slow breaths.

Grandpa took the mask away from his face and Mick said reluctantly, 'I shouldn't have shown you that picture, Grandpa.'

'And happen maybe you should an'all!'

Grandpa sat up a bit straighter in his chair and smoothed his hair with the flat of his hand. It was a thing he did when he was thinking hard and it gave the impression that he was squeezing out thoughts and that it was a very painful thing to do.

Grandpa carried on with his stroking and smoothing, and after a while he said, 'Maybe I should tell you how it happened round here, before it goes wrong in the history books, or you get it cockeyed from somebody else.

'You see, up until the time of the strike the miners were run by Arthur Scargill, and he was like God to them miners up north, he couldn't put a foot wrong whatever he did. But then he up and asks us all to go on strike and the miners round here just didn't agree. They had memories of the time before and they weren't none of them for the strike at all. They wouldn't go along with Scargill and stop work straight away no matter how many times he told them to – so he sends his blokes down from the Yorkshire pits and tries to stop us going in – and that's when things take a turn for the worse. It got that nasty round here you dursn't go out. There were blokes scrapping and fighting up by the gate, and folks chucking stones and bottles and worse. I'm telling you, it was a scene from hell and I hope never to see the like again. Them blokes Scargill sent were called Flying Pickets and they had a lot to answer for, our Mick. It was like a madness got into us all at the time and I were no better than the rest of them – you *wanted* to have a go at Scargill's men, it was bloody warfare every day and that's the way it was just then.'

Grandpa stopped for a moment to catch his breath. Through the rasping noises he made, Mick could hear a different kind of noise, a clashing, thumping, shouting noise; the striking of metal and the thud of stones. It was a sound like a medieval battle raging, straight from the history books at school. It was the sound of blood and guts and hate and it made Mick shiver although the room was warm.

Grandpa's breathing was as ragged and harsh as the voices he could hear, but the mask helped to bring it back under control. When Grandpa was breathing properly Mick said, 'So what happened in the end then, Grandpa?'

Grandpa wound the tube carefully round the plastic mask and when it was all neatly rolled he said, 'Well, we couldn't stick with Scargill's lot after that, so we formed a union of our own. His lot were called the National Union of Mineworkers and that gave us all a bit of a laugh – there were nowt much national or union there. So after a think we came up with a name and we called ourselves the Union of Democratic Mineworkers, and that had a better ring to it. We felt happier with a name like that.

'But it's an ugly business, Mick me lad, to see men fight like they fought just then. It stays with you like a permanent scar – there's no real dignity in fighting like dogs at a time when there's enough for all to go round.'

Grandpa stopped his talking all of a sudden and gave a long, deep sigh. It was as if the sigh was blowing away the brutal past like sucking the poison out of a wound. Then he gave himself a little shake. 'Now then, son, I've said all I'm going to say about that, so you can stop looking at me like a flaming dead sheep and give me a hand back into bed.'

Mick took the picture away from Grandpa and put it face-down on the windowsill. He wished he had been able to draw something else, something bright and soothing to cheer Grandpa up, but his wishes did not seem to count for much. For some reason Mick felt profoundly guilty, as if he were to blame for Grandpa's past.

When Grandpa was tucked up again in bed he said, 'Shall I put that picture up on the wall, or do you want me just to chuck it away?'

'You'd best put it in its proper place – I doubt there's anything worse to come.'

Mick carefully Blu-tacked the picture up and then stood back to have a better look. None of the pictures were what he had wanted to draw, except, perhaps, the boy with the horse, but now that he had them in front of him he could see the history that was taking shape.

The past was more than just a tale to tell, it was the truth about his grandpa's life.

For a long while Grandpa did not speak again, and when he did, he startled Mick. He said, 'It'll not be long before you're gone from here.' And the way he said it he was stating a fact as if everything was nicely cut and dried.

'You what?'

Mick stared at Grandpa as he folded his hands together over the sheet. He looked very smug and pleased with himself.

'You're better at drawing than anything else – and you're a damn sight better than with the cornet. It stands to reason you'll have to go – how else d'you expect to get on?'

'It beats me how you pick up on things!'

'Aye well, blood's a lot thicker than water, our Mick, and there's not just you with ideas in your head – but before you hop off could you get us some fags? I could murder someone for a snout or two.'

'Don't be daft – our Mam'd go mad if I did – and any road, what about me and cornet?'

Grandpa screwed up his eyes and tapped his nose. 'I've me spies on the lookout same as everyone else.' He gave a chuckle that turned to a wheeze, and at the same time reached across for his mask.

Before he put it across his mouth he said, 'If I were you, lad, I'd forget about music! If I were you, I should stick to art!'

It was true that Mick was not a natural musician – but the march was the thing that kept him working all those hours with Charlie Binns. It was the one thing he was determined to crack, even if he never did anything else. On the day that the pit was finally closed, there would be a Brown going out with the rest of the lads. The band and the pit were Grandpa's life; it was up to Mick now, to see it through.

10 Truant

The band and Doris. They were like two beautiful tunes playing in harmony. Doris in the field with her apron full of damsons and the rich, dark sound of the band. Doris's laugh was in his head: 'Kiss me! Go on then, don't be shy!' He could hear it again and again in the dark, 'Kiss me', like a cool stream running through his brain. Did Doris know how scared he was? Or did he fool her like he fooled the rest?

He was leading two quite separate lives and maybe one of them was a lie, but was it the one down here in the dark, or was it the one up there in the light?

It was odd how you could dream about something and the dream would turn out to be more real than life. Mick's head was filled with Grandpa's joy and pain and his own life was gradually being squeezed out into a thin, uncertain shadow of how it really was. Dark clouds swirled and eddied at the back of his brain; it was only by exercising enormous control that he managed to keep them at bay.

And now Mick was tired. He was tired, and he was angry as well.

He had the idea that Grandpa had repressed his true feelings all his life and they had never been reduced to a normal, manageable, everyday size. Without actually deciding to, or having any apparent choice in the matter, he was acting as the narrator and sounding board for Grandpa's life. It was as if Grandpa was waiting for him to depict what was in his mind and on Monday morning when Mick woke up he decided that he had had enough.

Today Mick wanted to forget about Grandpa. Today he wanted to be himself.

In a minute his mam would call him downstairs. Mick got out of bed and pulled on his clothes. When he looked in the mirror to brush his hair the face that looked back at him was pale and tight. His eyes had a mean and sullen look and Mick was scared by what he saw. Up until today he had thought that it was other people who got angry and violent; not him. He was the artist and the sensitive one. But today it was as if he was suddenly creating rage and pain without any help, and he could not stop it from breaking out.

In the kitchen his dad was eating toast and reading the morning paper. He did not look up when Mick walked in, but read the paper with great concentration. There was a frown between his eyes, and the frown and the paper seemed to shut Mick out.

'What do you fancy – do you want an egg?'

Mick's mam was holding an egg poised ready and a pan was steaming on the stove. Mick shrugged his shoulders. 'I'll just have some toast.'

'That'll not see you through the day!'

'I'm telling you I don't want an egg! You never listen to what I say!'

'That's enough, our Mick! You'll have an egg and you'll stop acting up like some great daft lout.'

Mick glared at his mam. His rage was simmering very gently and the egg was like some strange, potent symbol between them. But Mick did not want to fight with his mam so he focused his anger on the egg.

'I don't want an egg! I don't like eggs! What I want is to get away from here! I'm sick to death of everything! I want to be an artist now! I want to go to college!'

Mrs Cotton carefully lowered the egg into the pan, and his dad folded the newspaper up into a neat little square and placed it at the side of his plate. It came to Mick that his dad had been caught out by the sudden silence and did not know what was going on. Now he scraped his chair against the lino and looked surreptitiously at the door.

'Well then.' Mick's mam settled her back against the wall and folded her hands across her chest. 'I don't know what I'm to say to you, Mick. We've been through this college thing before.'

'And you never said I could go and do art!'

'I've never said as you *couldn't* go – but I want you to make something of yourself and get a job as'll see you through life.'

'I don't want to lead your kind of life! I want to go away and study art!'

'I don't know where this is coming from, Mick, and I haven't got time to deal with it now. But eat up your egg and we'll talk again later.'

'I don't want to eat the flaming egg. I want to . . .'

'. . . go off to college and study art!'

Mick's dad finished the sentence for him and Mick looked to him for help. But instead of help, he intercepted an expression that just for a moment was serious and cold, before it relaxed again into its normal everyday ordinariness.

Very softly his dad said, 'I know what it is you want, our Mick, but I'll not have you upsetting your mam like that. Now eat your breakfast and get off to school before I say something I'll regret.'

Mick ate his egg in silence, but a monster was in the middle of taking him over. A monster that was larger and more complex than anything he had experienced before.

He finished his breakfast and went outside without bothering to say another word. The sun was shining over Haddon Terrace, bleaching the brick to a pale shrimp-pink. Mick turned his back away from school and set off for the station.

The station was at the edge of the village. There was just a platform and a concrete shelter with a timetable protected by a sheet of glass. At that time of the morning the platform was deserted. There were tickets and cigarette papers blowing about, and across the line, the tomb-like trees clambered up the side of the heap.

When the train came in Mick sat at the back, hunched against the window. Nobody spoke to him. None of the passengers came near to sit. The Midlands landscape went rolling by and somehow it looked harder and bleaker than it had looked before. Pylons and telegraph poles marched away across the fields; there was nothing in the country-side to soften Mick's mood.

110

At the terminus he got off the train and headed up towards the town. The town was busy for a week-day morning. There were market stalls at the side of the pavement and crowds of people milling around.

Mick walked on slowly. Now that he was here he felt oddly dislocated, as if parts of him were breaking off. All of the people were strangers to him, marching along like soldier-ants. He felt in his pockets. Fifty pence. Hardly enough for a cup of tea.

Suddenly Mick was filled with despair. Everything seemed so hopeless and impossible to achieve. He would never leave Bilston; he would never be himself. The rest of his life would be spent living vicariously through someone else.

He leaned against a lion in the Market Square. The lion was made out of rough, white stone and Mick could feel the claws digging into his back. In the distance he could see the castle looming high against the hard blue sky.

Mick stared at it. The castle looked solid and familiar and real. Everything shifted and changed about, but the castle was always reliably there.

And now the castle seemed to pull Mick on. Up the lane and over the hill. The clear spring sun had brought out the shoppers; people with brollys and bags and cases. Everything looked very calm and still.

But when he got to the castle there was no one there. The chairs round the bandstand stood in straight, empty rows, and it was too early in the year for the ice-cream van. Mick leaned on the wall. From where he stood he could see the town: spread out in front of him were factories and shops and toy-town houses with the ribbon of river winding through. Mick followed the line of it with his eye.

People *did* sometimes manage to get away.

Mick saw that quite clearly with half of his mind while the other half went whirring on: what would happen if he *did* leave Bilston? What would happen to the folks left behind?

Slowly he turned round. The castle grounds were dressed for spring. There were huge round beds of hyacinths giving off a deep-blue scent, and the stiff regularity of the flowers was at odds with the torrid jungle-smell. If he had some paper Mick would sketch the flowers as prim maiden aunts with fancy drawers.

Mick was looking at the flowers quite calmly – and then suddenly he wasn't. He was shouting at the top of his voice and sobbing hard along with the shout: 'I'll go if I want to – d'you hear? Don't think you can flaming well keep me here!'

He drew back his foot and kicked at the flowers. One, two, three of the hyacinth heads were gone and he was cavorting through them kicking and shouting and waving his arms like a wild man.

It was the snapping noise that made him stop.

The hyacinths had such thick, green stems. The snapping noise was like a pistol sounding at the back of his head.

Mick stopped where he was and looked around. All across the soil the hyacinths were kicked and strewn about. The toes of his shoes were wet and shiny with the sweet, sticky ooze of the sap.

Suddenly it was intensely quiet. Mick felt sick with grief and shame. Until today he would not have believed that he could do such a wicked, destructive thing.

Very slowly he made his way back to the path. For some strange reason his head was clear.

Mick walked down the path and through the gate. People were gathering on the cobbled slope and standing around in little groups. There was a bus with a banner in the window which read: NOTTINGHAM WELCOMES BARENTON.

He put his hands in his anorak pocket and breathed in deeply. There was a peculiar feeling in the pit of his stomach, and suddenly it gave a giant lurch. He managed to turn his back to the crowd and lean out over the castle wall before he was hugely and abruptly sick.

Mick's dad was waiting for him when he got home, and that was unusual in itself. His face had that funny, carved look again, as if it was hewn out of a big piece of stone.

Mick did not attempt to say anything. He put his bag down on the floor and took his anorak off. And all the time he was doing it he was conscious of his dad's hard, rock-like presence waiting silently for him to sit down.

When he was sitting at the table his dad said, 'Well then, Mick. What have you to say?'

Mick shrugged his shoulders and looked down at the table. He could see every knot and swirl of wood and every separate speck of dust. His tongue felt swollen in his mouth. How could he explain what had happened today? What could he say that would not sound soft or stupid or a lie?

The clock ticked on the dresser; outside the window the sun dropped in the sky, leaving a swirl of orange cloud. Then Mr Cotton cleared his throat. He said, 'You see we had this phone call after you left, from one of your teachers up at the school. He wanted to know if you were taken ill, and I was pressed to know what I should say.'

Mr Cotton did not look angry. His voice was as serious and calm as his face. It did not seem to belong to the Dad Mick thought he knew, the one who was quick with a laugh and a joke. Then Mick fetched back a memory from when he was little. He was at the seaside with a bucket and spade. He remembered how the sand felt rough like warm salt and the weight of the bucket full of thick, brown water. And then a smaller kid came and took hold of his spade. There was the sense of rage boiling up like an angry sea and Mick walloped the kid on the head with the bucket. Mr Cotton's face had had the same look then. Not angry or vengeful or even unkind. But a serious, considering, judging look.

Mick wanted to tell him all that had happened, but he was stuck as to how to even begin. In his mind Grandpa, art, Paul and the pit were all hopelessly entangled. Somehow, and without knowing how or why, they seemed mysteriously to have become the same thing, the same burden, the same precursor of some terrible doom, and he could not begin to explain what had happened to him.

He looked at the table helplessly and his dad started speaking to him again.

114

'You see, Mick, we've started to worry a bit about you. We know you're growing up and want some space, and maybe we've kept you on too tight a rein. But it's more than that, isn't it, son? You don't seem happy any more and we can't seem to fathom the reason why.'

Mr Cotton sounded so puzzled and hurt. And the hurt was worse than anger would have been. Mick could deal with anger, but he was often a disappointment to himself and he did not want to disappoint his dad.

He was wondering about the best thing to say, when Mr Cotton said suddenly, 'Is it Pa upsetting you, Mick? You've been a bit down, like, since he came to live here. I know you feel more than other lads, but I don't want you getting upset about Pa.'

'It's not just Grandpa – it's more than that!' Mick found himself shouting and he stopped in surprise. He hated the sound of his own loud voice; he did not really want to go on. It all seemed so impossible now, his feelings were so indefinite and vague, it was the *sum* of them that was weighing him down. But Mr Cotton was waiting, and his face all at once was very kind.

Mick said slowly, 'It's just, I get these feelings, like. As if I'm living in someone else's head. I seem to feel all the things that they feel and it makes no difference if it's good or bad. It's like my head's wide open to everyone else's thoughts and fears, and once they come there's no turning them off. Right now it's Grandpa and I don't mind that, except I never knew how unhappy he was, and I can't get away from what's going on unless I make it into art. Sometimes I think I don't exist at all except in someone else's mind – and that's when I start to get really scared. This morning I wanted to run away and try to get back inside my own skin.'

Mick finished what he was trying to say and then stared down at his hands. He had not managed to tell the half of it, he had not mentioned the outburst in town, and his fears about what might happen to Paul.

But Mr Cotton was sitting back in his chair and his face had a careful, considering look. He seemed to be weighing up possible courses of action and sorting exactly what he should say. When he came to a decision his eyebrows twitched back from the bridge of his nose. It gave him a more settled, homely look.

He said, 'Now listen here, Mick. You're my lad and I'm not one to go about shouting the odds, but you're a very special sort of bloke. I'm not too sure of the ins and outs, but maybe other artists are like you. It's my idea you've outgrown us here. You need different people who know about art to try and show you how to go on. I know you're upset about your Grandpa, but to my mind there's more to it than that. You need folks who can talk to you about what you do and I reckon I've just come to realise that . . .'

He paused for a moment, and Mick drew a deep breath to have his say, but Mr Cotton held up a hand at him: 'Hang on a sec, I'm not finished yet. You shall go off to college as soon as you can, and you've my word as I shall see to that, but – and listen close to what I say next – I'll not have you upsetting your mam. You have to remember that Pa's her dad and she's going through a bad patch now. This skiving off . . . I know what you say and I believe you, Mick, but I don't want it to happen again.'

Mick felt his face go very red. The redness seemed to creep up from the soles of his feet and spread out through the rest of his body until his face was steaming hot. He said, 'I won't, Dad, honest I won't! I didn't actually mean to before, it just happened and it won't again – and any road, I'm sorry about Mam. It's just . . .' Mick shrugged his shoulders and tried to choose the best thing to say. '. . . It's just, she's all the time wanting me to be different. She wants me to get through life like her, just being sensible all the time.'

'And that's how it is for most folks, Mick! That's mainly how it's been for me! Not everyone has got what you've got, you know, though I had some ideas when I were a lad. Hang on a sec, will you? There's sommat I've got you might as well see.'

Mr Cotton left the table and went upstairs. Mick could hear him rummaging in cupboards and drawers, and in a minute he came back into the kitchen with a brown paper envelope clutched in his hand. The envelope was large and old and grubby and covered in cancelled orange stamps. Very carefully his dad ungummed the flap and took out a bundle of thick white paper. He turned the paper round to Mick.

The papers were pictures of all shapes and sizes. They were pictures of houses and people and places, and they were executed with extraordinary clarity and power.

Mick studied the pictures one at a time. He could not believe what he was looking at: a whole vivid slice of exuberant life was spilling across the kitchen table – and his dad had not mentioned them up until now!

Mr Cotton said slowly, 'You see, I had some ambitions when I were your age, but art was mainly for pansy-boys then. I hadn't the nerve to keep it up and now it's come out again in you.'

Mick stared at his dad. He had thought it likely that he took after Grandpa, and now here was his dad springing this on him!

He said shyly, 'It's rotten that you didn't get the chance to go on, but I reckon you're smashing the way you are.'

'Aye, well . . .' Mr Cotton put the pictures back into the envelope and very firmly sealed down the flap. Then he gave himself a little shake. He said to Mick, 'Well don't just sit there looking dumb! Give me a hand with the tea things, will you – quick, before your mam gets back!'

When Mick went to bed he could not sleep, and he lay for a while, staring into the dark. It had been a day of best and worst: his dad had helped to sort things out, but at the same time had somehow muddled things up. Mick's art seemed much more important now. Now, there was his dad's lost past to consider – and what if he went and let his dad down?

Mick thought things through. Soon, he knew, he would leave Bilston. He would do what his dad and his grandpa said. He would go somewhere to learn about art.

But for now the march was getting closer. In a week or so's time the pit would shut; the band would strike up when the miners came out, and he, Mick, would really be there.

He'd be marching along with Grandpa's best mates. He'd be blowing away as loud as he could. He'd be making Grandpa proud of him. He'd be doing his best to march in Grandpa's shoes.

11 The battle

A trip to Limbo and back again. He named the pit Limbo in his mind;
he made his fear into a place he would only visit from time to time. It
was a place full of dark and secret spaces that he could decide to
leave when he wanted to. And outside the place there was a splinter
of light. The light was like an open door, and behind the light there
was a different place; a place he had never seen before.

He imagined the sun hanging low in the sky, and it was a different
sun to the one he knew . . . it was bigger and lighter and more full of
warmth. And beneath the sun there was a different world . . .

The day after his trip to town Mick was back at school again. The
chat with his dad had not really helped; when he got out of bed his
stomach was churning and he did not want to go to school.

Grandpa was dying and Mick was afraid. If Grandpa died what
would happen to him? Mick was living Grandpa's life – so if Grandpa
died, would Mick die too?

And at school there was an atmosphere. It was more than the

excitement of the march and the coming closure of the pit. Kids were standing about in little groups. Mick could see them whispering with their heads close together, and they looked at him oddly when he walked in. Mick saw the way they were bunched together, but he could not be bothered to push his way through. His head was still bursting from the dream he'd had; it was a dream of dust and noise and dirt. The noise was a rolling clap of thunder that rushed through his head like the surge of the sea. If he could draw out the thunder Mick's head would clear; the thunder would be black rolling cobbles of coal, Mick would push them and pummel them over the page, he would use his fingers like a brush.

Mick leaned his back against the wall and watched a kid come sauntering up.

'Hey-up, Mick Cotton.'

'Hey-up yourself.'

The kid was called Martin Shore and Mick had seen him around the playground before, although he was not in Mick's own class. Martin was standing directly in front of him and circling the ground with the toe of his shoe. Mick stayed where he was. Martin's body cast a shadow between them, and there was a gap for a time when nobody spoke.

Then after a while Martin half-looked up. His toe stopped its circling and there was a sudden hush. Out of the corner of his eye Mick could see the other kids moving together and forming a circle, watching them from a safe way off.

'Is it true about Paul?'

Mick was startled. 'You what?'

'You know what I mean. About his dad.'

'Oh, that!' Mick shrugged his shoulders. 'Yeah, I s'ppose. His dad was the one got coshed on the head.'

The boy dumped his haversack on the ground. There was a drawing and a rhyme on the side. The rhyme said:

> Mary had a little dog
> She kept it in a bucket
> Every time a dog came past
> It always tried to knock it over.

'I don't mean that, I mean the other thing. It was in the paper. His dad was in it – he got carted off by the fuzz yesterday.'

And that was the day Mick had gone into town.

He had a sudden flash-image of his own dad frowning over the morning paper; of Paul's new jeans and the sweater with stripes. All the loose bits and pieces of the last few weeks clicked neatly and grimly into place. Paul, and the way his mam had acted. Paul being kept away from school.

'Piss off.'

'What?'

'Piss off, go on.'

The kid stared at Mick, and his face had that baffled, spaced-out, blank sort of look you get when you are taken by surprise.

The other kids moved a bit closer in.

'You're mad, Mick Cotton. That's what you are.'

'And Paul's my mate, so watch your mouth!'

'I reckon he's fallen in love with Paul!'

There was a giggle from one of the girls in the crowd.

'Who's a fancy Nancy, then?'

Martin Shore did not want to fight, Mick could tell that from the way his flesh seemed to go very soft. It was nothing you could actually see, it was the essence of fear that Mick picked up.

His own fists began to clench in his pocket.

'Fancy Nancy, tickle-me-fancy!'

There was a chant from the crowd, quite low at first, but then louder as more people took it up.

'Fancy Nancy, tickle-me-fancy, Mick's a bit of a fairy-o!'

The kid stepped back a pace and Mick moved in. He was afraid all at once of Martin's fear; the fear made Mick remember his dream.

'Do him one – go on – stick one on him!'

'. . . Mick's a bit of a fairy-o!'

When the kid moved again Mick drew back a fist. In his nightmare Mick could see arms flailing and waving about. There was a moaning sound that filled his head and voices shouting behind the moans. Mick had the idea that if he did not try to fight, he would be trapped for ever in the dust and dark.

'Fancy Nancy!'

Uncertainly Martin looked at Mick. In the shadowy space between them Mick saw a white shape move, and he hit out at it as hard as he could. His fist made contact with soft, white flesh; he was clearing a way through the dust and dirt until the flesh burst open like a soft, ripe plum.

The blood on Mick's hand was warm and sticky. It had a sharp, metallic taste, like the yellow taste of his cornet. Mick was hitting out with his sticky hand; he was fighting the darkness inside his head; he was beating his way towards the light, when suddenly his throat went tight. His collar hurt and he could not breathe.

'Mick Cotton! You come with me! And you, lad, wait outside my door.'

Mick could feel the hairs on Mr Brierly's hand tickling against the side of his face. Mr Brierly was walking with a long, easy stride, and Mick was forced into a run to keep up with him. Across the playground and through the hall. The hall was a moving blur of pictures and Mick's feet were slithering on the floor.

'In here, lad.'

Mr Brierly's room was stuffy with the windows closed and the heater on. There was a desk in the corner piled high with papers, and an ashtray full of elastic bands.

'Stand where you are, lad, and don't try to move. I want to have a look at you.'

Mr Brierly tipped back on the legs of his chair. And then very calmly and coldly he looked at Mick.

'Well, lad. What have you to say?'

Mick lifted his shoulders and looked at the floor. The way he acted was rude and surly, but he did not know what he could say. Mick wanted to get back to the Mick he was, but it was as if that door was closed for good and he was forced into being someone else.

'You know what you are now, don't you, lad? You're a bully-boy and you're a thug. So – are you going to answer me or stay looking daft? Or maybe I'd better talk to your dad?'

'No!'

'Well then, lad, what have you to say?'

'Nothing much. It were my fault it happened. But they were on at me about being a Nancy, just because I stuck up for Paul!'

Mr Brierly tipped back in his chair again without bothering to speak to Mick. He just raised his eyebrows and nodded slightly and waited for him to carry on.

'Paul's dad got nicked for doing the raid – at least, that's what the other kids say. And now Paul might not be coming back and . . .'

Mick stopped where he was and considered a bit. Up until today, although he had thought of Paul as his mate, he had not been clear about what that meant.

But what if Paul did not come back to school?

There would be no one for Mick to pitch up against; no one his own age to reflect who he was.

Only how to explain all that out loud?

Outside the window Mick could hear the sound of voices singing. Then there was a gap and the scraping of chairs; some more music and then 'Bright Eyes'.

Mick did not know what to tell Mr Brierly – and besides – he was sick of explaining himself.

'Well, lad – are you going to carry on?'

'No, sir.'

'No, sir! Is that it? Is that all you can say to me? How am I supposed to help you, lad?'

Mick shrugged again. 'Dunno, sir.'

'No, sir! Dunno, sir! Well, Mick, I've a letter here in front of me and it's a letter from your dad. It's telling me you played truant from school, and it's telling me things are hard at home – am I right, or am I wrong about that?'

The letter was a big white square on the desk. Mick could see the handwriting upside down, but he could not make out what it said. He stared at the paper in disbelief. He was amazed at what his dad had done without so much as consulting him.

Now Mr Brierly said more quietly, 'Your dad's doing his best to help you, Mick. He's worried about the way things are and he wants to let you have your chance – and I'm right along beside him there. I want to get the best for you, but I'll not have you turning into a thug.'

Mr Brierly put his chin on the tips of his hands. Beneath his elbows the letter rustled and cracked. Then he carried on in the same quiet voice, 'Now then, Mick, if you can't seem to talk about how things are, I want you to start to write it down. I want you to put into words what's really to-do – you've been a good lad, Mick Cotton, up until now – I don't want you to spoil things for yourself.'

'I can't do that!' Mick found his voice. 'Writing's not sommat as I do! The way I work is, I draw things out – I'll not be able to write for you!'

126

Mr Brierly was already standing up. He was shuffling pieces of paper together at the same time as he was talking to Mick. Over the shuffling noise he said, 'This isn't a punishment for you, Mick. It's something I think might help you a bit – and, yes, I know you can draw, but for now I want you to write things down.'

Mick did not try to say anything else. When he went outside the school was settled into a busy quiet. There was a buzz from the hall where the mural was, and through the door Mick could see quite clearly the shape it had taken. If you looked at it from a long way off, the lines and angles and curves had a power and a presence they lacked close-to. Close-to you could see the joins and the stupid smiles on the too-pink faces. It was the sort of work that would impress his mam; she would know the number of pieces it took, she would be able to recognise what was what: it was the sort of work she would call art.

Charlie said, 'You're not trying for me tonight, are you, son? You're off somewhere else, and maybe a postcard'ud get there quicker!'

They were in Charlie's front room, and Mick could not manage to find his puff. Whenever he tried to play a note his thoughts would take off somewhere else. His head felt like a crowded room, with different thoughts jostling for space.

'I'm sorry, Mr Binns. I've one or two things need thinking about.'

'And so have we all, son, so have we all! But music's one as won't stand for that. It doesn't like taking second place. When you take up an instrument you've to give yourself to it body and soul – and

127

that's the thing as makes good music – if you can't do that you can pack it in now.'

Charlie was sitting on the arm of a chair. His belly was bulging over his belt and his trousers were shiny and stretched too tight. If his mam could see Charlie the way he was now, Mick could imagine the sort of sniff she would give: 'All beer and no brains,' was something she said, and yet somehow Charlie still gave off power. It was more than just conducting the band. Charlie was so *sure* of who he was; he fitted so snugly inside his own skin.

And Mick still wanted to march with the band!

Mick was struggling with himself and Charlie was quietly watching him struggle; letting him work things out for himself.

Now Mick said again, 'I'm sorry, Mr Binns. I'll have another blow and give it me best.'

'You do that, son. Whatever you've got that's troubling you, you channel it into the notes you play. Think about that and have a go, and we'll make a bandsman of you yet!'

Mick wiped the cornet with his handkerchief and then tucked the handkerchief into his pocket. He felt calmer and more settled than when he started.

'Now try me an F and then an E. Give it everything you've got in your head and I'll be boggered if you don't give me sommat good.'

Mick anchored himself more firmly on his feet. He believed implicitly what Charlie had said, and yet his head was still filled with darting thoughts. There was his dad and Paul, his mam and the kid.

There was Mr Brierly telling him to write, and there was the woman at the main pit gate.

Mick drew a deep breath and closed his eyes. He concentrated as hard as he could. He tried to make his misery into a tangible thing; something you could taste and touch. Mick's mind was blank and empty at first, but then a change began to take place, the thoughts which had been idly floating around eddied and swirled and gathered strength. Without knowing what had made it happen, Mick's thoughts came out of the instrument in one long, glorious, deep-blue note.

'You see what I'm talking about now, kiddo? Music *knows* when you're giving it your best. It's a living thing is an instrument, and you've to treat it with a proper respect.'

Mick was packing the cornet back into his bag. In two weeks' time he would march with the band, and that would mark the end of the pit. He wondered briefly what would happen to Charlie, and if the band would carry on. At the back of his head he could hear Grandpa's voice: *It's love, not money, as keeps a band going. You think on that a bit, our Mick.*

Mick said, 'I'll be off now, Mr Binns. Shall I see you tomorrow?'

'Aye, you will that, lad. I want you to bring up me gooseflesh again. And any road, you don't have to hurry off – I'll see if the missus'll let us out for a beer.'

Mick grinned at Charlie. In spite of the things his mam had to say, there were worse folks to be than Charlie Binns. If Mick had to choose to be someone else, he would fancy a go in Charlie's skin.

* * *

When Mick got home there was the doctor's car. He went in the house and put his cornet down on the table. His hands and feet were freezing cold, but he did not want to go into the living-room, and he did not want to go upstairs. He made himself a mug of tea, as much for warmth as the need for a drink. Grandpa was taken badly again, and everything Mick had wished for himself suddenly seemed foolish and absurd. Mick wrapped his hands round the mug of tea, but he could not manage to make himself warm. What was the use of all this trying? What was the use of wanting things when in the end it came to this?

The floorboards were creaking in Grandpa's room, and the kitchen was growing dark. Mick waited where he was on the hard kitchen chair, and soon there were footsteps on the stairs.

His mam was talking, and then his dad. The doctor had what his mam would call a real, nice, educated voice. It was the sort of voice that was not loud or strident, but which carried in a way his dad's did not.

The doctor was talking to his mam: 'He's as comfortable as I can make him now, the drug should give him a breathing space. Try not to worry too much tonight, and I'll call and see him again tomorrow.'

His mam murmured something in reply. There was the click of the door; the doctor's footsteps on the pavement, and then the sound of him driving away.

Mick sat with the cornet on the table in front of him. Behind the smell of supper cooking and the horrible whiff of disinfectant, there came a faint beer-and-smoke sort of smell; a smell like the bar at the

130

Dog and Duck. The smell was on Mick's jeans and hair. It reminded him of the men talking: *Us miners, we were the aristocrats! We were top of the heap of the working-class – and now we've to come out wi' cap in hand!*

Mick had sat in the place he usually sat with his back propped up against the wall.

Aye – there's some as say they don't blame Ken Reeve – to go from being what he was, to be a night-watchman like a dog on a chain. That's criminal if you was to ask me. That's not sommat as a bloke should do.

That's the beer talking, that! Ken Reeve weren't never no aristo-crat! If you want to set someone up for that, you've to look no further than Gil Brown . . .

Mr and Mrs Cotton came into the kitchen. Under the fluorescent light they both looked very pale. Mrs Cotton had a hand up to her face, half-covering her mouth and eyes. She was still wearing her office clothes; a pin-striped skirt and soft white blouse. Above the hand her eyes were flickering; she glanced at Mick and back again; she looked at the dresser with its shiny blue plates and at the clock with the bills poking out behind. And when she had finished her gazing around, she settled her eyes on the radio.

'Is our Grandpa taken very bad?'

'Aye, son, he is. But the doctor's trying out this new drug, and it'll likely ease things up for a bit.'

Mrs Cotton settled herself down at the table and nodded across towards the cornet. 'Don't think you can give up learning that thing – Pa'll still be here to see you march.'

'Can I go up and see him now?'

'I should leave it tonight, son. Pa's a bit weak with all the fuss going on, and you know what he's like when his temper's up.'

'I bet he gave that quack a do!'

Mr Cotton gave a short, sharp laugh. 'He did an'all, sick as he was! When the doc put a hand on his bare chest he said, "You can take them bloody fish-fingers off and fetch me up a bit of sommat hot!" '

He laughed again, and Mick joined in. Then after a second his mam laughed too. The three of them sat round the table and laughed and laughed. Mick felt closer to his parents, in spite of Grandpa, than he could remember feeling for a very long time.

When he got up to leave the room, he turned in the doorway to say goodnight. His mam and dad were still at the table, and Mick could see that they were holding hands.

12 Crisis

Doris knew about his fear, but she did not understand the shape of it.
She said, 'Only a fool would not be scared to take himself down pit.'
Doris thought his fear was like her own fear: it was a fear you could
talk about and make sense of; a rational thing you could understand.

But his fear was infinitely greater than that. It was more terrible
and more dangerous than anything he had to compare it with. His fear
was a beast that snarled at his back, and he could hear it roaring
again, even over the sound of trucks and his own voice singing. There
was an ominous, distant, dark sort of noise, like the giants he had
read about when he was young. The noise seemed to swell and grow,
and go on growing until his head was filled with its terrible roar. He
had the sense of the world tilting and turning upside down; his lungs
were filled with bitter dust, the darkness had a blacker pitch now.

Gil thought, I'm going to die, and with the thought came a strange
sort of calm. He could almost see the rank spoor of his fear as it
slowly and silently oozed away. He closed his eyes and settled back,

but through the dark he heard a voice; the voice was calling out to Gil: 'Help me! Gil! Oh God, help me . . . Please . . .'

Mick wrote, *I think my grandpa was afraid of the pit for nearly all of his life.*

Then he stopped for a moment and considered. The thing he had written seemed disloyal somehow. The cold, hard words in some strange way made a lie of Grandpa's life; of the vast, throbbing, colourful whole that Mick could not begin to put into words.

He tried again. *Grandpa carried on going down the pit, even though he was so afraid. And when he came up he played with the band.*

Words were not the same as art. Mick could not shape them into the pictures he wanted to make for people. Once they were on paper the words looked too stark and mean and definite. They made a statement folks might actually believe because they were written down.

Grandpa played the solo cornet. He was very popular with his mates.

Nothing. The words said nothing about Mick's grandpa. His life was contained inside Mick's pictures. His fear was a shrieking explosion of dark, the cornet was a piece of fine old gold, and Doris a gentle stream running through.

Mick stopped his writing and put down his pen. The marks of the picture he had made last night were still visible on his fingers. The charcoal had bedded down into his skin and rubbed itself into the clean white sheets. Mick's room was turning into a black disaster; there were charcoal marks on the chest of drawers and on the wall-paper nearest to the bed.

Mick's picture was propped against the wall. In the grey of the early-morning light the cobbles and shale and swirls of dust were like a huge black beast devouring the page. If he stared at it for more than a minute he discovered that he could not breathe; the charcoal and dust and hard black coal seemed to get into his mouth and eyes.

Mick had the idea that Grandpa was there somewhere, under the monstrous collapse of coal, and that he had suddenly gone very quiet and still. He drew the quietness as a long, dark tunnel opening out into a field of light. It was like being drawn into a pool of absolute peace and quiet. Looking at the picture made Mick want to sing and shout and dance about.

The pictures were both a beginning and an end, and somewhere waiting in between, there was still the woman at the main gate. When he opened the drawer, Mick could clearly see the shape of her face through the layers of tissue paper. Over the last few days the face had got stronger, and more definite; it had a luminous quality that it had lacked before. And yet in his hands the picture felt very light and thin; he could almost see through it to the rubs of charcoal smeared on the wall.

Mick stared at the woman, and the woman stared back. Today Mick would hand her over to Grandpa. Since Grandpa had taken badly again the house had become peculiarly quiet. People were tiptoeing around each other and speaking in low, unnatural voices. It was as if Grandpa's illness had set him apart, as if it had managed to rub him out; as if Grandpa had become a child again.

But Grandpa was not a child. He would hate being treated the way he was, and today Mick would show Grandpa some more of his life.

When Mick finally went downstairs, his mam shot him a swift, disapproving look. She said, 'You've been at it again, I can see by your face.'

His dad said, 'Leave it be, will you, Mam?'

'Sorry I spoke!' Mrs Cotton said. 'I suppose I'm not good enough for art!'

Last night's closeness had disappeared. His mam's face looked puffy and pale and lined, and it was likely that she had not slept. If they had been different sorts of people, Mick might have given her a hug, but as things were he said very softly, 'You're the one as lets art happen. You're the one as looks after us.'

'Aye, well.' Mrs Cotton looked pleased without actually showing it on her face. Changing the subject she said to Mick, 'I'm sorry about that Paul of yours – will you go and see him sometime today?'

'I'll go up after school tonight, but it's likely his mam won't let me in.'

'She's a lot to put up with, has Brenda Reeve, and maybe she's better without her bloke. I was going to tell you there's a pie in the pantry if you want to go and take that up.'

'That's grand of you, Mam, and ta – I will.'

At school things were back to normal again. Nobody avoided Mick or gave him funny sideways looks. It was as if the fight had broken a spell and Paul was part of the class again. People were talking about him openly: what would Paul and his mam do now? How would they manage on their own? And, would Mr Reeve get sent to prison?

Mick allowed himself to be drawn in.

'What do you reckon, Mick?' asked Sally Tomms. 'D'you reckon as Paul will come back to school?'

'Don't see why not – it weren't his fault.'

'Right – and it wouldn't have happened at all, I bet, if pit hadn't had to go and close down.'

'Aye – Paul's dad would have been safe if he'd stayed with the pit.'

'You tell him he's welcome to come back to school.'

Mick was astonished. Before Mr Reeve got caught by the police, Paul was someone who was simply *there*: Paul Reeve, nobody special, just carrying on being his usual self – only now that his dad had done something wrong Paul was almost a hero.

'You tell Paul he's to come back here and not bother himself what folks might say.'

'My mam says he can come round to us and maybe have his dinner.'

The class was drawing a wall round Paul, and Mick was oddly jealous. He wanted Paul to come back to school, but *he* wanted to be the one who protected him. He did not want Paul to belong to the others – because what if Paul preferred them to him? Bilston had a way of pulling together if anything happened to one of their own; there was a chance that Paul would be swallowed up and Mick would be left without a friend.

At assembly Mr Riley made an announcement. The Lord Mayor was going to lead the march. '. . . You should be pleased and proud when the men come out. You should think on what kind of men they are and the life they gave to Bilston village. You should be glad you've been a part of that . . .'

No doubt Mr Riley's words were true, but they gave Mick an ache deep down in his guts. Bilston still had one foot in the pit and there was no great agreement about what would come next.

After school Mick made his way round to Paul's. The weather was still very soft and spring-like, and there was a red blade of sun behind the trees. Mick pushed his way through the fence at the back. The dog was asleep in his wooden box; there was washing hanging on the line, and the tub of water was still by the door. The water looked black in the evening light and the house was dimly reflected in it.

Mick stared at the strange, distorted shapes. He had the idea that everything was in its usual place, but that the landscape had somehow subtly changed. Everything was different; the colours were softer, and the trees had got rid of their skeletal look – they were gently fuzzed over with pale mint-green.

He knocked at the door and it opened quickly.

'Well, I don't know! It's our Mick come to see us – will you have a sandwich while you're here?'

Mrs Reeve spoke as if nothing odd had happened, and Mick felt foolish with the pie in his hand. Awkwardly, he gave it to her. 'Me mam sent you this. She says to let her know if there's owt she can do.'

'Bless me! Whatever next, young Mick? You're to thank your mam very much from me – we shall have this pie for supper tonight.'

Mrs Reeve put the pie down on the table and gave a yell for Paul. When Paul came in he was wearing old clothes. He looked his usual scruffy self. Nothing he was wearing belonged to his dad.

Paul grinned at Mick. 'Hey-up me old mate – d'you fancy going out for a bit?'

'He won't have a sandwich, Paul, he looks too thin – and don't you be late back here for tea.'

'I shan't be long, Mam. I'm just out for a bit.'

'Aye, well then, bring us a cabbage if you go out back.'

Paul nodded and closed the door behind them, and they walked on down the path. The sun was laced with thin white cloud and the soil was runny and squelched on their boots. For a while, neither of them spoke. Then the lights of the pit flickered on in the distance and cancelled out the glow of the sun.

Mick said, 'I'm sorry about your dad and that. What will happen now, d'you think?'

Paul shrugged his shoulders and kicked at a stone. He did not seem to mind Mick's questions.

'Nothing much. Not until it gets to court. They've got him banged up in the nick for now and the police came over here today. They went through the house looking for cash, but they didn't find it and they went away.'

Mick stared at Paul. It was like listening to a story from one of his books. Mick was amazed that Paul could act so calm. He tried to imagine how he would feel if his own dad had been slammed in the nick. The idea made his blood run cold. He could imagine his mam's appalling shame; the way she would abruptly shut up shop, and the way she would depend on Mick.

They carried on walking very slowly, and suddenly it was properly dark. A train shrieked a long way down the line and with the dark came a dank sort of chill.

Mick spoke again: 'So what'll you do? Will you come back to school now, d'you think? Now that you're not so needed at home?'

Mick wanted Paul to come back to school, but he did not want to explain to him everything the other kids had said. Mick did not want Paul to have other friends – and, besides, he was mad at Paul for being so calm. It was not natural to be calm like that.

Paul put his hands under his arms. He said suddenly, as if he had read Mick's thoughts, 'It's easier at home without our Dad. He was for ever going upsetting things. Our Mam'll get benefit now he's gone and she reckons we shall manage all right.'

Mick did not reply. They were on the allotments behind the house and the sky was a hectic sulphur colour around the pithead. There was the smell of cabbage and rank vegetation; a sudden scurry through the grass, and then the scut of a rabbit's tail.

Paul cut a cabbage from the end of the row and tucked it in the crook of his arm. He said, 'I reckon I'll be back tomorrow. I don't want to be missing when it comes to the march.'

'Will you try to march instead of your dad?'

'Aye – if they'll have me, and I reckon they will – it was the pit, any road, as did for our Dad.'

Paul's face was flickering yellow and white from the arc-light reflected in the sky.

Mick said, 'Right then – I'll see you tomorrow, maybe.'

'Yeah – I expect – and ta muchly for coming round.'

When Mick got home the house was bright. Every light was blazing out and all the curtains were still drawn back.

His mam called out from the living-room, 'Is that you out there, our Mick? Did you remember to take the pie? And is poor Mrs Reeve all right?'

'Yeah, she's fine – she says to thank you for the pie.'

'Good lad.'

His mam's voice was muffled by the radio, and after she had had her say she turned the volume up again, and Mick could hear her start to sing along.

13 Heroes

Mick went up to his room and opened the drawer. He took out the picture of the woman and the picture of the coal. Then he set them carefully side by side. Mick had meant to study the pictures, but as soon as he did so there was a strange rumbling noise. Inch by inch the room grew darker. Grotesque shadows flickered and writhed and made black patterns on the wall. Soon the room was densely black; there was not a hint of light, even when his eyes grew used to the dark.

And that was when the voices came.

Oh Jesus! Help me . . . Help me . . . Please . . .

Gil . . . are you there? Hold on me old mate . . .

Jesus . . . Doris . . . help me . . . help . . .

Mick shrieked. And then stopped abruptly with his hand to his mouth. He was not sure if the shriek had come from him, or if it had come from some other source. There was a heavy weight across his chest. The weight was pressing down harder and harder. Mick thought that his chest would collapse under the terrible crushing weight. He had a sudden nightmare picture of his ribs and stomach caving in; the spurt of blood and the splinter of bone.

He closed his eyes. The weight made it impossible for him to breathe. There was a deeper blackness coming now, and the weight was lighter on his chest. Mick knew that he was going to die, and that it did not matter any more. He knew that he was starting a journey, and the journey was long and very hard ... that he was moving purposefully and with great speed towards a distant, glowing sun ...

And then the light was suddenly snapped on.

Mick's mam was standing in the doorway. When he opened his eyes there was a blur of white and a blur of grey. He found that he was hunched against the wall with his knees pressed tightly against his chest. He blinked, and the room came into focus. His mam was looking at him with large, scared eyes.

'What's the matter, Mick? Have you taken bad?'

His mam did not touch him or move in close; her voice sounded very shrill and light.

Mick made his arms relax by his sides. He could see the way his mam's eyes were drawn to the pictures on the dresser. He sensed that she was balanced on the edge of panic and at any moment might erupt herself. With a great effort of will he found his voice.

'I were just having a bit of a lark about and I fell against the wall.'

The thing Mick said sounded hollow and untruthful, and his mam did not believe it. Mick could tell that from the way her eyes swivelled towards him and stayed there a minute, before they went back to the picture of coal.

'Aye, well . . . just mind what you get up to in here.'

His mam waited a moment, still and silent, looking at the picture of fallen coal. And then she turned on her heel and left the room. Mick could hear her going down the stairs, the tap of her feet on the lino floor, and the definitive click of the living-room door.

Cautiously, he straightened up. His legs were aching and his chest still hurt. When he touched his eyes they were gritty and sore. Mick could not remember what had happened. There was a vague idea of something immense and powerful and awe-inspiring that had suddenly given way to light.

He looked at the pictures again, and this time his eyes were drawn to the woman, but now Mick was certain who she was. For a long time he stared at her soft, pale face. He had the notion that she was smiling faintly, and that the smile had superimposed itself over the fall of coal.

She knows me, he thought. And I know her. He could not believe he had been so stupid as not to recognise his own grandma. Even though she had died so young, she was still a part of Mick's own flesh and blood.

Blood's thicker than water, our Mick, you'll see . . .

He took up the picture and went out of the room. There was a faint spit of light under Grandpa's door, and without bothering to knock Mick went straight in.

Grandpa was propped upright in bed against a towering mound of pillows. The pillows smelled of soap powder and starch; they were stiff as planks and aggressively white. Mick could imagine his mam arranging them; the way her hands would hammer and punch them into the right sort of shape. One day Mick would draw his mam as a pair of hands, and the hands would be square and busy and capable. Mick's mam's grief came out of her hands and that was another thing Mick had learned.

'You're here then, are you?'

Grandpa's voice was gravelly, and quieter than Mick had heard it before.

'I've brought you a couple of pictures, Grandpa.'

'Have you now? I thought you might.'

Grandpa did not sound particularly grumpy. He sounded as if he *expected* Mick.

Mick moved a bit closer to the head of the bed. He noticed with a shock that the cornet was back on the bedside table, and that it was a bright, gleaming, unblemished gold.

He put a picture on the bed, and it was the one with the massive fall of coal. Mick did not say anything. He just handed Grandpa his spectacles and waited while he put them on.

'I knew somehow it would be this.'

Grandpa had the picture close to his nose and was studying it quite calmly. It occurred to Mick that Grandpa had lived through the pit disaster not once, but a second time more recently inside his head, and that the second time Grandpa's pain and trauma and hideous fear had somehow communicated itself to Mick. And now that fear had burned itself out. Mick's picture was simply a record of what that fear had been.

Grandpa wiped his spectacles on the edge of the sheet. He said to Mick, 'You see, I've had these bloomin' queer waking dreams to do with you and Doris and the coal. It seems to have straightened me out a bit – and so maybe I'd better explain myself.' Grandpa put his spectacles back on. Behind them, his eyes looked startlingly large and blue. He said, 'Pull up a chair, will you? There's a good lad. It gets on me wick to see you stand up.'

Mick pulled up a chair as close as he could and put his feet on the snowy bed. Grandpa flashed him a look and grinned a bit, then he picked the picture up again and slowly carried on.

Grandpa said, 'The day of the fall I was feeling queer, but that was always the same with me. I'd fancy I could hear a noise and that's what came of being so scared. But then comes the day it really happens . . .

'There was a rumbling noise from a long way off – it sounded like a chuffing train – and I expected it was just me head, so I carried on, on me hands and knees. And then . . . there was so much of it, you see, bloody coal was everywhere. You'd never believe there was that much coal . . . and the noise . . . it was an evil, rumbling curse of a noise. It was like listening to the end of the world.

'And afterwards, when the coal's come down, there's this other noise and it's deep in your head. You feel like it's a part of you, only you don't rightly twig just what it is. It's a muffling, deafening sort of noise – and it's silence, Mick, that's what it is. It's a silence like you can't imagine – like nothing you've ever heard before.

'Then I could hear someone screaming in the silence, and at the bottom of it all I knew it were me – but I were listening, if you take my meaning – as if I were listening to someone else. I were listening to them shouting and moaning and praying, and then all at once I knew Doris was there.

'She'd gone over, d'you see, to the main gate, as soon as she heard the terrible news, and she was talking to me inside her head and willing me to stay alive.

'You can feel it, you know, Mick, when somebody cares. I can't rightly explain to you just how it is – it's a queer kind of force that gets inside you and helps you to find the strength to cope . . .'

Grandpa stopped for a moment and reached for his mask. To Mick's mind he was not breathing into it deeply enough. He could see Grandpa taking short, shallow breaths instead of the long ones he usually took. But then Grandpa put the mask away and folded his hands across the sheet. For a long while he did not say anything else, and Mick was afraid he might have fallen asleep. Very gently, he began to ease his feet away from the side of the bed.

'You needn't think you can bogger off now!'

Grandpa was glaring at him from the depths of the pillows.

'I'm only trying to stretch me legs!'

Mick put his feet back on the floor and then picked up the picture of Doris. He studied it for a moment. It might have been his imagination, but she looked quieter, somehow, and more composed. The tense way she had looked when she first emerged seemed to have softened a bit around the edges; Doris looked happy and tranquil now.

You're daft, Mick told himself. It can't do that. But he knew that in some strange way, it had.

'Give it here, lad, will you? Let me have a look.'

Mick handed the picture over to Grandpa. For no good reason he felt extremely tired. His eyelids were drooping and his muscles ached, but for the first time in weeks his head was clear.

He saw Grandpa stroke the picture very gently, tracing the lines of the soft, white face. Doris was Mick's maternal grandmother – so was she anything like his mam?

Mick was thinking about that when Grandpa said suddenly, 'I was in an air-pocket and I was panicking and I reckon maybe I was halfway dead, when all at once I heard Doris talk. She was talking to me like I was standing there – and suddenly, I was calm again. It were like a miracle, I'm telling you, I were calm as owt and me head was clear. I could hear another bloke calling out, and the sounds were getting lower and lower. I had this idea he were behind me somewhere and I began to scratch at the coal with me hands.

'What I'm telling you is, I'm lying there near flat on me back and I'm scratching the coal from behind me head! The coal was slithering on to me chest and I was afraid there'd be another fall. Then all at once me hands touch flesh, and that's a miracle I'll never forget . . .'

Grandpa's voice trailed off, and he passed a hand across his face. Mick understood that Grandpa was gone for the moment, back to the pit, back to the moment which changed his life.

The picture fluttered in Grandpa's hands.

He said slowly, '. . . We both got out. We both got out and we were alive! And Barney (that were the name of the man I found) kept saying as how I'd saved his life! Me, Gil Brown, the one who was always so flamin' scared! And do you know – they say as things allus come in threes – another miracle was on its way. When I went down pit a few weeks later I found, God help me, that I wasn't scared!'

Mick took hold of Grandpa's hand and squeezed it hard. He had the sense that something amazing had happened to both of them. Grandpa's past was nearly finished, and the pictures were arranged in chronological order all round the bedroom walls. Mick took up the picture of Doris and the picture of the fall, and Blu-tacked them nearest to Grandpa's bed. Now that his head was clear again he could look at the two pictures separately: the face of Doris and the face of the pit. The one seemed to bring the other into focus; Doris had been proud of Gil, and that pride shone out from the bedroom wall.

'There'll never be her like again.' Grandpa was nodding at the picture of Doris, and Mick saw quite clearly that she *was* special, and that she had indeed saved Grandpa's life. But out of the blue came a burst of anger: Grandpa had not been able to love his daughter as much as he had loved his wife. He had made no secret of that fact. Mick's mam had been a lonely child and part of that was Grandpa's fault.

He said fiercely, 'Our Mam's the one as looks after us all. I want you to understand me right – our Mam's a special person too!'

Grandpa gave a loud crack of laughter that turned into a wheeze.

He clamped the mask back over his face. When his breathing was steady he took it off. He said to Mick, 'It don't take a lot to get you going, I can tell you that much for a fact – you're a regular chip off the old Brown block!'

Quick as a flash Mick said in reply, 'And there's a fair old bit of our Dad in me, too!'

'Aye, so there is, and I reckon you could do worse than that.'

Grandpa picked the cornet up off the table and held it between his hands. He held it very gently, as if he was weighing it on a balance.

'Here lad, you might as well have this.'

'No, Grandpa – I can't take that!'

'It's no use to me, son, any more. And besides – I've heard a whisper as you're doing well.'

'I'm not doing as well as I ought to be!'

'I daresay – and maybe none of us do that. Go on – take her, lad, and give her a bit of a blow for me.'

Mick took the cornet back to his room and put it on the chest of drawers. He had the idea that things were not finished yet: that there was another picture he would have to do.

Mick tore a page from an exercise book. He wrote on it: *Today Grandpa changed for good from being someone who was always scared into an almost-hero.* And then he paused for a moment, thinking hard. When he took up his pen again he wrote: *I've been living with Grandpa's terrible fear and now the disaster's finally come, and in a weird sort of way it's released us both.*

Mick was satisfied with what he wrote, but there was something

nagging at the back of his head: if Grandpa was a hero after the fall –
did that make Mick a hero too?

14 The dream

Gil was dreaming. The dream was not like his usual dreams; half-waking, fretful visions of the sound and fury of the pit. This dream had a clarity and lustre that Gil had experienced only occasionally in his life.

Gil was dreaming of wide green spaces. The spaces were lit by a sun that did not dazzle but gave out a clear, white light. In the dream there was a stream, and Gil was sitting beside the stream, listening to the sound of water bubbling over tiny stones.

He knew that he was dreaming. He was aware that he was standing outside his body and watching his other self in the dream. The dream-person saw his life reflected in the water. His life rippled past in front of him: the land, the pit, the terrible fear like a fathomless spread of black in the water; and Doris.

Doris was smiling. Gil could feel the strength of Doris's smile, although he could not properly see it. He was smiling back, and his own smile was mirrored in the water, which changed from a clamorous burst of colour and sound to a clear, gentle flow. Gil saw himself walk towards the flow. The water was drawing him gently in. He was eager to step into the cool, clear water.

But all at once Gil heard a note. It was a long, deep, golden note, and he waited, and listened until it had gone. The note was important somehow to Gil; it reminded him of something he had to do. He waited until it was quiet again, except for the water over the stones. Then he gave the stream a last, long look, and slowly drew back from the edge.

15 The march

Mick sat up in bed and blew a note. It was six o'clock in the morning and not yet properly light, but for some reason Mick had woken early. He lay where he was in the warm pit of his bed, and stared at the pictures on the ceiling. His curtains were not drawn across in the middle, and his room was filled with a strange, white, luminous light. Through the light he could see the flowers he had painted a few months earlier, and he had the notion that they had somehow changed. They were not the same, hot-house, foreign flowers that had rampaged across the hint-of-peach. These flowers were soft and yellow and small; they flowed across the ceiling in an unbroken stream.

Mick stared at the flowers for a very long time. It was the day of the march, and he had expected to wake up full of excitement and fear; but instead there was this strange sort of calm. Mick did not want to get out of bed; his limbs felt deliciously warm and light. His whole body seemed to relax and dissolve into the soft warm depths of the bed. Mick wanted to stay where he was for the rest of the day, and simply fall into a long, deep sleep.

But the light outside grew brighter. Mick picked up the glint of Grandpa's cornet reflected on the bedroom wall. The cornet made a luminous puddle of gold, and slowly and reluctantly, Mick sat up.

When he played a note, the note sounded richer and softer than it had sounded before. Mick had the idea that he was hearing it from a long way off, and that somebody else was playing it for him. He put the cornet back on the table and waited for his mam to appear. He expected her to throw open the door and grizzle at him for waking her up. But nothing happened. The room settled back into its early quiet, with just the sound of the birds outside and the milkman clanking bottles.

Mick closed his eyes to savour the quiet. Without knowing why, he was sure that Grandpa had heard the note, and that it was a special bond between them.

The night before, Mick had washed the cornet in warm soapy water. He had buffed up the brass to a magnificent sheen and then put the cornet on the bedside table. Mick had tried to settle down to sleep, but he could not make his mind go quiet. Every time he closed his eyes there was a confusion of noise and flickering pictures. The pictures washed through his head like a tumbling stream and the sensation was eery and disturbing, but it was not frightening or sad.

And in the end Mick had got out of bed. He had taken his sketch pad out of the cupboard and set it on his lap. The paper was very white and clean, but now that it was in front of him, Mick did not know what he wanted to draw. The pictures he saw inside his head were reeling past at an impossible rate. It was like watching a video speeded up; there were snatches of the band and snatches of the pit; guns and rabbits and instruments; the grey-blue smoke of the Dog and Duck.

Mick was impatient for the pictures to stop. He had the pencil in his hand and he was filled with an urgent need to draw. He waited, tapping the pencil on the edge of the pad, and very soon the flow slowed down. Mick saw a stream with a young man in it. The young man was laughing and kicking up the spray, and in the spray there was another face.

Mick drew the faces with great sureness and speed. He drew Gil and Doris. The music Gil made flowed along with the bubbling stream, and Mick almost felt himself drawn in. His head was very light and clear, and his body was weightless and invisible, as if it was made out of pure, clean air.

Mick laughed out loud, and immediately with the laugh he felt the weight of his own flesh and blood. His arms and legs were amazingly heavy and clumsy and hard to move. Very slowly, he lifted his hands and rubbed them across his face. Today he could not afford to be ill. Today, of all days, there was so much to do.

Mick got up from his bed and went to the window. The pithead was etched against the grey morning sky. Cold, hard angles and lines. Rivets of steel and that terrible wheel. Mick stared at the pit. The pit was a monster that had gobbled men up, but at the same time, it had given Bilston life.

The picture Mick drew was on the bed.

Gil and Doris. Doris and Gil.

Their story was almost finished, and before he went to school that morning, Mick would put the picture on Grandpa's wall.

Carefully, Mick covered the picture with tissue paper, and then he got dressed and went downstairs. At nine o'clock he would be at school and the morning would be spent preparing displays. Now that the mural was finally finished, the classrooms were being tidied up, and more work was being tacked on to the walls. At lunch-time there would be a break, and then the march from the pit would begin.

Mick's mam and dad were in the kitchen, and the first thing Mick saw was a miner's hat placed by his chair at the table. The hat was a dusty orange colour with a dent in the side and a crooked lamp stuck near the brim.

'What's that doing there?'

His mam glanced round, and Mick nodded at the hat. Mr Cotton was behind the paper.

'Your grandpa thought you might wear it, like. It's the last one as belonged to him.'

'Oh.'

Mrs Cotton looked at Mick more closely. Her face was faintly pink and her hands were gripped together.

'He wanted you to have it, Mick, and maybe wear it for the march, and Mick – he hasn't long to go.'

'I know he hasn't – but I'm not wearing that.'

'Now, Mick . . .'

Mr Cotton rustled the paper closed. He made a long, noisy business of it, and when he had folded it into a single neat square he said, 'Hold on, our Mam, and let Mick have his say.'

They both turned to look at Mick.

'Well then, son?'

Mick stared at the hat. Now that he was being asked to explain, he could hardly find the words. He simply had the feeling that the hat was a trap, and the wearing of it would be a lie.

But his mam and dad were waiting for him to tell them what was on his mind.

Mick took a deep breath. He said, 'I never was a miner and never shall be. I'm marching for Grandpa and what he was – and I'm marching for what he might have been. The way I see it, I'm marching as much for what's to come as for what's been left behind – and that hat – it only says one thing. It says the pit's all that counts and that's not true, so I won't go having it on me head.'

When Mick had finished there was a sudden quiet. Then his mam puffed out a long, troubled sigh. She said to him, 'But Mick, you have to think . . .'

'. . . As he's a bloke as knows his own mind!'

Mr Cotton grinned at Mick and stuck the hat on his own curly head. It was a size too small and perched ridiculously over the tops of his ears.

'Take it off, our Dad – you look right daft in that!'

'I always said you had a big head!'

Mrs Cotton was laughing and her hands were unclasped.

'It looks like a blooming pea on a bun!'

'Oh, don't mind me – I've no feelings to hurt!'

Mick glanced at his mam. 'Will you be coming to watch the march?'

Mrs Cotton's hands were abruptly together again and her fingers were weaving in and out. She looked at the radio, and then back at Mick.

'I shouldn't rely on it, our Mick, not with Pa the way he is. I'm taking the TV up to his room and maybe we'll watch the march together . . . I'm feeling like I shouldn't leave him, you see.'

'Yes . . . right . . . OK.'

Mick could not stop himself from sounding surly. He knew that what his mam said was right, but he still felt disappointed. Mick had worked hard for the past few weeks, learning to play an instrument. He had learned it for Grandpa and all that he was, and Mick wanted his mam to understand that. He was afraid that the television would make it unreal – that it would turn into just another show.

Mick looked at his dad. 'Dad?'

'I'll be there, son – and I'll be wearing that hat! Now – give us a hand with the telly, will you? I can't manage myself up all them stairs.'

They lugged the television up the stairs and set up the indoor aerial. Dad kept up a flow of chat:

'Move it this way . . .

'No, lad . . . not so far.

'The aerial goes in here, I reckon.

'So what have you got for your snap today?

'. . . I reckon you're doing better than me . . .'

It came to Mick that his dad was chatting to cover the sound of Grandpa's breathing. Mr Cotton did not look at Grandpa, but busied himself with plugs and stands.

When he was finished he went downstairs, and Mick moved across to Grandpa's bed. Grandpa was propped up against the fierce white pillows, and he had his eyes shut very tight.

'Grandpa – I know you're not asleep.'

Mick touched him gently on the shoulder, and after a second he opened his eyes.

'You know more than is good for you!'

'Aye, Grandpa, no doubt – but I've got another picture to show.'

Grandpa snapped his eyes shut tight again. The sigh he gave was like a rusty saw rattling against an old piece of wood.

'You've got in the way of me dreams, young man. That picture had better be bloomin' good.'

Mick grinned at Grandpa's closed-up face. 'It is, Grandpa, so don't go looking like that. I'll go and fetch it – hold on a sec.'

He went out on to the landing. From downstairs came the sound of the radio and his mam singing along: '*Blue moon* . . .' Mick took the picture off the bed. Like the pictures on the ceiling, and the picture of Doris, it seemed to have somehow changed again. It was thinner and lighter and more luminous than it had been before.

Carefully, he carried the picture to Grandpa's room, and without saying anything, he fastened the spectacles on to Grandpa's nose and then held the picture in front of him.

'You can open your eyes now, Grandpa.'

Grandpa opened his eyes very slowly and stared at the picture. He let his eyes wander across it in a leisurely fashion. And then he let out a long, deep, rattling sigh.

'By gum . . .' he said.

The picture appeared to Mick to be reflected, very delicately, in Grandpa's face.

'You like it then, Grandpa?'

'Like it? You're drawing me blooming dreams now, Mick! Like it? You know flaming well I do!'

'Yeah – well – I'd better tell you now, I s'ppose – I'll not be wearing that stupid hat.'

'Oh, won't you now?'

Mick lowered the picture on to the bed. He had a notion that Grandpa was enjoying himself, and that he was not really mad.

'I can't wear it,' he said, 'because I'm not really you. I'm meself, that's who I am – and besides – it makes me think what you might have been.'

'And what might that be then, young man?'

'Anyone, Grandpa!' Mick shrugged his shoulders helplessly. 'You might have been anyone, that's what I'm saying! And I'm me, Mick Cotton, I'm not really you!'

Grandpa reached for his mask and breathed into it lightly. When he had finished, he gave a sharp tap to the back of Mick's hand. He said, 'Now you just listen to me, our Mick. I like you for what you said to me, it's sommat I might have said meself . . . You mustn't let anyone tell you who you are . . . you just be sure who you are yourself.'

'Aye, Grandpa, I know. I'd better be going – shall you be fit to watch the march?'

'I'll see you on the telly, Mick – so don't forget to give us a wave!'

'OK then, I'll be off.'

Mick made a movement and then came back. He did not want to leave Grandpa. Very gently he took hold of his hand. Mick was amazed again at how soft it was. It was like a hand belonging to a lady; a lady who did not do any work.

'So long then, Mick.'

'So long, Grandpa.'

Mick went downstairs. The tune on the radio had changed from 'Blue Moon' to 'Tulips from Amsterdam' and his mam was singing and stacking the dishes with a lot of clatter and noise.

He picked up his bag. All it contained was Grandpa's cornet.

'I'll see you later then, our Mam.'

His mam did not stop her singing. She nodded at him, and ran some water into the bowl.

When Mick got to school, Paul was there. He was being fussed over by some of the other kids, and he looked pleased and sheepish at the same time.

'Hey-up then, kiddo – you made it, then?'

162

Paul edged his way to the fringe of the group. 'Looks like it – and any road up – I wouldn't miss the march for owt.'

Paul had a plastic bag in his hand. Through it, Mick could see the shape of a miner's hat. Paul did not play an instrument, but he was going to march instead of his dad. Just for a moment, Mick felt a short, sharp, pang of regret – maybe, after all, he *should* wear the hat? But then he remembered Mr Reeve: rabbit's corpses in a dripping row; the terrible temper of the man . . . And the way he cracked without the pit . . .

'Hey . . .' Paul dug him in the ribs. 'Looks like we shall be on the telly. Good job I'm wearing me second best togs.'

Outside the school railings, a large grey van had arrived. On the side of the van it said, *B.B.C. Television Outside Broadcast.*

'Cop a look at that, will you? We're going to be famous!'

Kids were swarming up to the railings and shouting to the van:

'Would you like to snap me where I am?'

'I can do an interview if you like.'

'I'm a lot better looking than her . . .'

'Yer blooming well like the back end of a bus . . .'

Mick hung back on the edge of the crowd. It was like Carnival Day in Bilston village; bunting was strung up along the main street, and folks who usually stayed in bed were up and dressed and walking about. Even the sun seemed high in the sky. It glanced off the roof of the bicycle shed and struck sparks off the asphalt in the playground.

Inside the school it was unnaturally tidy. The walls were all decorated with work, and in Mick's classroom his own work was set apart from the rest.

Mick glanced at it. Technically it was quite efficient, but it was like a book with the text ripped out. Something vital was not there.

'It's not your best work, I'll grant you that – but it will impress the hell out of the folks who come here. Now – did you manage to write anything down for me?'

Mr Brierly was standing behind him. He had come up silently on rubber-soled shoes, and he seemed to be able to read Mick's thoughts directly through the back of his head.

'My real work's at home on Grandpa's wall – it wouldn't be right up in the school.'

Mr Brierly nodded, and folded his arms. 'Well then – apart from that – and *did* you manage to write anything down?'

Mick fished around in his anorak pocket and drew out a piece of paper. The things he had written seemed stiff and trite and terribly untrue. He handed the paper to Mr Brierly, 'This here's not what I want to say. You'd have to see me real work to know what's been to-do.'

'Maybe I could do that one day, Mick?'

Mick nodded awkwardly. 'Yeah. I expect. One day you will.'

In his pocket there was another piece of paper. Mick had written that morning: *Today's the day of the march from the pit, and Grandpa won't be there.*

The rest of the morning was spent tidying up and chaffing each other about the march. At eleven o'clock there was a special assembly, and Mr Riley stood at the front. Mick could tell that he was enjoying himself. Cameras were popping while he spoke; the hall was strung about with wire and special dangling microphones. Mr Riley was wearing a gown with a hood, and he hooked his thumbs into his lapels. He looked like a small, proud cockerel balancing on the soles of his shoes.

'. . . and so I tell you this is a new beginning . . .

. . . Bilston stands proud in the history of coal . . .'

Mick flicked in and out of Mr Riley's speech, and at half-past twelve he left the school and set off by himself for the pit.

Smoke was hanging in the still spring air, and along the route the march would take crowds were beginning to gather. Mick walked fast and steadily and did not stop or break his stride, even when folks asked about Grandpa.

Hey-up young Mick – so how's old Gil?

He's not very good, ta, Mr Daws.

Give him me best when you get back home . . .

When he got as far as the main gate the crowds were thicker and jostling for space. There was a banner up on the railings that read: BILSTON MINERS R.I.P. and another television van was parked outside.

Mick stopped for a moment and looked at the gate. Under his coat, the cornet pressed hard against his ribs. Mick hugged his arms across his chest. For some reason he was suddenly very cold; his flesh felt starved of warmth and blood. When he looked at the gate with the pit behind it he saw a huddle of grey-faced women. There was a sudden flash of Doris's face, a searing pain across his chest, and then the picture vanished again.

Behind the railing, Charlie waited. He was busy counting in the band: 'Twenty-one, twenty-two . . . Three more to go – now then, Mick, you'd best come in and I'll show you where you have to stand.'

Charlie looked magnificent. His uniform was scarlet with gold epaulettes and frogging down the front. A scarlet stripe ran down his leg and his boots were polished to an icy shine.

'Over here, lad. I want to have a word with you first.'

All of the band were wearing scarlet. The way the sun shone down on them it was as if the land outside the gate was suddenly set on fire. Boots were stamped against the ground, instruments clanked and clanged and gleamed; drums gave out an occasional roll.

Mick was awed, in spite of himself. The scene was like a picture he had looked at once in the castle museum. The picture was called 'Before the Battle' and it gave off the same powerful sense of expectation. It made you think of sweat and blood, of horses pawing at the ground and swords being clashed to make sparks fly. If he closed his eyes Mick could hear the yells and smell the sour-sweet horses smell.

'Are you going to stand gawping all day long – or are you going to come along with me?'

Charlie took Mick firmly by the arm and marched him into a little room. The room was some kind of disused office, with a notice-board and a sagging desk, and battered chairs against the walls.

Charlie's huge red presence overflowed the tiny space, and Mick pressed his back against a chair.

'Now then, Mick, so how are you?'

'I'm all right, Mr Binns. Grandpa's not so good.'

166

'I know that, Mick, but you listen here.' Charlie puffed his cheeks out into a big round balloon, and then gave Mick a very serious look. 'You're not to worry about your grandpa. Where he's going I reckon he'll be OK – just do your best when it comes to the march, and the rest will somehow take care of itself . . . And now, young man – hold on a sec. Muriel's sent you up something she's made herself – if I can only remember where the hell it is!'

Charlie was bending over the dusty desk with his giant buttocks in the air. He was rummaging through the battered drawers and Mick could hear him muttering to himself: 'I put it here, I know I did – or did I put it in this drawer? I've too much to think about, that's what . . .' And then he finally gave a yell, 'Here it is, where I thought it was! Thank God for that – I had an idea I might have to go home!'

Charlie wafted a hand in front of his face and handed a parcel over to Mick. The parcel was wrapped neatly in stiff brown paper secured with a piece of stout white string.

Mick took hold of the parcel. He was baffled as to what could be inside – it was not his birthday, and it was not Christmas – so why should Muriel give a present to *him*? He started to undo the knots in the string, carefully, a knot at a time, and Charlie shouted and looked at his watch, 'Come on, Mick, will you? Get a move on, lad. We haven't got all day, you know.'

Mick ripped the last of the paper off. Inside the parcel lay a tunic. It was scarlet and gold with shiny brass buttons, and on top of the tunic there was a note.

The note read:

Have this as a good-luck present from me. It belonged to Charlie when he was a lad – and as you can see, he's grown since then!

I hope it fits (I had to keep hugging you to get your size – and because I've a bit of a weakness for lads!). Hope I've made Charlie jealous a bit – if not, he'll get the flat of my hand!

Good Luck, Mick, love.

Yours, Muriel.

XXX

'And here's me thinking she fancied you! Mind – like she says – any excuse to get hold of a lad!'

Charlie was reading the note over Mick's shoulder, and Mick felt himself go red in the face. He glanced up at Charlie and said very slowly, 'Thanks, Charlie. Thanks very much. And please thank Muriel from me.'

'You can thank her yourself. She's not done with you yet! Now bustle about lad, we're starting soon. Put your stuff in this here desk, and come outside when you're all fixed up.'

The tunic fitted Mick like a glove. He could feel the snugness of the material stretched neatly over his shoulders and chest. There was no mirror in the office to admire himself in, but Mick walked up and down as if he was marching, keeping time to a tune inside his head.

Suddenly he felt immensely proud. Whatever happened from now on, Mick had done the very best he could.

He opened the door and stepped outside, and straight away was engulfed in noise. The band were beginning to get into line and Charlie hustled him over to his proper place. He said to Mick, 'This is the spot where Gil would have been . . . Now don't forget what I just said. It's too late to worry about anything else, so shoulders back and stay in line!'

The Lord Mayor was ready to lead the band out. He stood at the front in a purple robe, and his chain of office winked in the sun. Outside the gate the crowd was waiting. They were quieter now, there was just a gentle, rustling murmur, and they were looking expectantly towards the yard.

And then all at once a cheer went up. The doors at the back of the yard were open and the miners were starting to walk on out.

Mick looked at the crowd. People were jostling each other to get a good view, and he wondered briefly if his dad was there.

But then the drums began their beat.

Boom! Boom! Boom-ba-boom!

And Mick lifted the cornet up to his lips.